screaming at the ump

screaming at the ump

Audrey Vernick

CLARION BOOKS
Houghton Mifflin Harcourt
Boston · New York

Clarion Books

215 Park Avenue South

New York, New York 10003

Clarion Books is an imprint of Houghton Mifflin Harcourt Publishing Company.

www.hmhco.com

The text was set in 13-point Norlik.

Library of Congress Cataloging-in-Publication Data
Vernick, Audrey.
Screaming at the ump / Audrey Vernick.
pages cm.
Summary: Twelve-year-old Casey lives with his father and grandfather at their family-run umpire school, and as he deals with middle school and his mother's unwelcome return, he stumbles on a sensational story that has him questioning his dream of becoming a journalist.
ISBN 978-0-544-25208-0 (hardback) — ISBN 978-0-544-30669-1 (ebook)
[1. Baseball — Fiction. 2. Baseball umpires — Fiction. 3. Single-parent families — Fiction.
4. Journalism — Fiction. 5. Fathers and sons — Fiction. 6. Mothers and sons — Fiction.]
I. Title.
PZ7.V5973Scr 2014
[Fic] — dc23   2013036213

Manufactured in the United States of America
DOC 10 9 8 7 6 5 4 3 2
4500472405

This one's for the home team — Michael, Jacob, and Anna —
who also happen to be the best cheering
section of all time.

screaming at the ump

Right Off the Bat

PEOPLE always assumed I was going to be an umpire when I got older, like my dad and his dad. Or teach at their umpire school, Behind the Plate. But the thing about umpires is, if they do their job well, they aren't part of the story at all.

Not that I wanted to be part of the story. I never wanted to be a player. Or one of those statistics-obsessed fans.

I wanted to write about baseball, to report on it, to show how every game is unique, its own unpredictable story.

And now I could finally get started.

It would all begin today.

* * *

Three eighth-graders I didn't know were shoving their way to the back of the bus. I ducked out of their way, sat down near the front, and looked out the window.

Middle school meant a school newspaper! I wasn't too excited about the other back-to-school stuff, but I'd always known this was when my life as a reporter would begin. I could finally write for a newspaper! I wondered what my first article would be, what headline would be over my first byline: *by Casey Snowden.*

When the bus reached Zeke's stop, he found me and practically sat on top of me as the bus lurched forward. I had kind of hoped he might take this opportunity—starting a new school—to make some changes. Like maybe remembering to brush his hair before he left the house. It always looked like a big pile of brown—not straight, not exactly curly, just big. I probably hadn't remembered to brush mine either— but that's easier to get away with when you have just plain straight hair.

Without even a quick hello, he started rambling on about some epic episode of *That'sPETacular,* where a kitten got stuck on a roof, and it was so hilarious, because there was a squirrel or something. It was one of those things that most people would realize wasn't going to be funny when you tried to tell it, but Zeke wasn't most people.

"And then at the end they made this announcement — I can't believe no one thought of it before — but it is so cool, and I am so going to win."

I was half listening as he rambled on about some new contest, called Your Show Here, where regular people submitted ideas for their own reality TV show. "Is that, like, an idea just made for me or what?" he said.

I couldn't even imagine where his brain would lead him. Zeke had always been obsessed with reality TV. Or, to be more accurate, somehow being part of reality TV. And he had a kind of overactive and maybe a tiny bit insane imagination. It was entertaining, being his best friend, without a doubt. It was never boring.

When we were nine, he was absolutely convinced that our mailman was really the first host of *That'sPETacular,* Joey Collins. I'm guessing you're ahead of me on this one — you probably already figured out that our mailman was not, in fact, Joey Collins. Over time, I'd figured out that I shouldn't believe everything Zeke said. But still, he was fun. And loyal. And we always found the same things funny (we were often the only ones laughing in a movie theater at any given time). Ninety-two percent of the time, I was glad he was my best friend.

We got off the bus, and when the school doors opened, we walked, with what felt like tens of thousands of other kids, inside. I pulled the orientation info out of my backpack — room 219. My homeroom.

As soon as the teacher had taken attendance, she let us go out to our lockers. I found mine, opened it, and hung my backpack up, after getting out the notebook I'd nabbed from the supply room at Behind the Plate last night. I closed the locker door and was about to head back to 219 when I noticed all the other kids were still turning their combination locks, some kicking at the locker or asking the kid next to them to help.

I guess most of them didn't live on a campus with lockers all over the place. I helped some kid I didn't know and these two girls, Leah and Marley, who were in my class last year. They all acted like I was some kind of genius for knowing how to open a locker.

The whole first day was all about learning to use our lockers and finding our way through the halls and meeting our teachers and writing down the supplies we'd need and blah blah blahing. Lunch was cool, I guess — it was good to see my friends again. But we got through the whole day without anyone even saying the word *newspaper* a single time.

On the afternoon bus, I was thinking about everything I'd missed by not being home today. I wasn't there when the staff arrived for our annual five-week

Umpire Academy, and I felt like if this bus didn't begin moving faster, I was going to jump off and start running.

Umpire Academy started tomorrow. It was as close as I came to anything like a family reunion. I never thought much about being an only child, because every September, it felt like I had about a dozen big brothers. A lot of the staff had been working at BTP since before I could remember. Some had regular names—Joe Girardo, Lorenzo Watkins, Hank Lorsan—and some everyone knew by their nicknames—Soupcan, Steamboat, Bobbybo.

During the rest of the year, BTP hosted all sorts of different clinics and classes for umpires to improve their skills, but there was nothing like Academy. It was the big one.

I couldn't wait to see those guys.

The bus was way too hot. And smelly. At the first stop, it took FOREVER for three kids to grab their backpacks and get off the bus, then one kid realized he'd forgotten his jacket—who needed a jacket on a sunny, eighty-degree day?—so he got back on and off again. Everything was like that—slow motion.

Zeke and I jumped up when the bus got near my stop. The driver yelled, "Siddown! No standing till the bus is at a complete stop." I tripped over Zeke and heard some snickers as we stumbled back to our seats like a pair of sixth-grade clowns.

When we finally got off the bus and rounded the corner, we jogged to the front gate, which was now left open, since Academy was in session. We walked down the long driveway, all the brick buildings laid out ahead of us like a small college campus. There weren't as many cars in the parking lot as there should have been. I didn't see one with Rhode Island plates—Steamboat must be running late.

We walked past the cafeteria and through the main building until we got to Mrs. G. (her last name had something like eleven syllables, and I wasn't even sure *she* could pronounce it), who ran the front office. She kept her dyed-some-unnameable-shade-of-orange hair knotted up on top of her head and often stuck pencils, pens, and I'm not sure what else in there, too. She called all the students Honey, and she called me Baby, and she called Zeke Zeke. Today there was some little girl with her. She was young, maybe eight. Really pale, with long black hair.

"Baby," Mrs. G. said, "this is my granddaughter, Sylvia."

"Sly," the girl said, embarrassed.

"Most people don't call me Baby," I said, embarrassed too. "I'm Casey."

On Mrs. G.'s desk there had always been this picture with the name Sylvia written vertically on the page, each letter starting a different word. I always got a kick out of the first two:

Smart

Yes, excellent.

(*Y* is a hard letter.)

I did the same project in first grade, but mine's not hanging anywhere.

"And this is Zeke," I said.

"Sly? Are you, like, a fox or a raccoon or something? What kind of name is Sly?" Zeke asked. I was thinking that someone whose real name was Ezekiel should probably not have been speaking at that time.

She nodded. "It's better than Sylvia, isn't it?"

I had to agree. I wished my name had a cool nickname. Or at least a nickname that would keep people from assuming I was a girl.

"How old are you?" Sylvia asked.

"We're eleven," Zeke said. "Which is quite old."

"I'm twelve," I reminded him. Like a lot of kids in Clay Coves with summer birthdays, my parents signed me up for an extra year of preschool, and now I'm one of the older kids in the grade. I like to hold that over Zeke whenever possible. "How old are you?" I asked.

"Eight," she said.

And then we made a quick exit because I did not want to be spending this day hanging out with Mrs. G. and her granddaughter. I had waited all year for this! I was dying to see everyone.

Preseason

WE found Dad and his dad (my grandfather, Pop), and Bobbybo setting up one of the classrooms, unstacking chairs and pushing desks around.

"Casey!" Bobbybo called, coming at me. There was this awkward "Do we high-five or fist-bump?" moment and then he just hugged me. He did the same to Zeke. "Where've you guys been?"

"School," I said.

"You're looking good, just like your old man," Bobbybo said. I glanced at Dad, whose hair was too long and who needed to shave, but otherwise, yeah. He did look pretty good for an older guy.

"Loose lips sink ships," Pop said. Usually what he said made sense.

Bobbybo shot a look at Dad, who gave a quick

shake of his head. Did they think I was an idiot? Or blind? Something was going on.

"What?" I asked.

"Nothing," Dad said, lining up desks evenly near the front of the classroom.

Were people coming later than they said? Dad and Pop hated that—not a good way to begin.

Usually, there'd be teams working in the different classrooms and lecture hall, but the building was quiet except for us. "Where is everyone?" I asked.

"Soupcan and Hank and Joe are out with the truck. And some are still on their way."

"What should me and Casey do?" Zeke asked. "Are the dorms open? Do you want us to make sure they're clean? Or the lecture hall? The cages? Tell me. I'll get right to work."

Zeke's parents were both kind of laid-back people, two very calm dentists, and Zeke was this sort of always-bouncing ball. I guess his parents were always in motion too, in a way—they both worked almost all the time, but it was like they walked and talked and, I guess, worked, too, in slow motion. Kind of like that guy Mr. Rogers, who used to be on public television. And they were hardly ever home. But Zeke's energy ... there really was nothing quite like it.

Pop was watching Zeke and shaking his head. "I'd like some of what he has," Pop said.

Dad laughed. "Casey, you and Zeke head out to the cages. Make sure the cameras are all working, the pitching machines, all of it."

"Right," Zeke said. "Excellent." You could probably tell him to scrub the toilets and clean out the goop at the bottom of the gym garbage pails and he'd thank you for the opportunity. I worried, not for the first time, about his parents' choice to name him something that rhymed—so easily!—with *freak*. And *geek*.

"Are you hungry?" Dad asked.

Zeke nodded.

"Okay, then. Let's all go eat something first."

"I'll keep working," Bobbybo said.

I knew there was, like, no food in the house. No one had gone shopping in a while. Even though it had been just the three of us for years, no one had yet figured out the grocery part of our daily lives. As we walked into the kitchen, Dad asked, "Casey, how are we for cereal?"

Cereal we had.

I pulled out three boxes and put them on the table. Pop got the milk. Dad grabbed some bowls, and Zeke pulled four spoons out of the drawer.

"Here's to a great beginning," Zeke said with a big

smile. We reached for our spoons, but he wasn't done yet.

(Pop couldn't wait. He snuck a spoonful into his mouth.)

"And here's to teaching fair and foul. Safe and out. And doing whatever it takes to get it done." He made us clink spoons before the rest of us could start eating.

✱✱✱

We were clearing the table when Dad said, "Casey, your mom called again."

I moved the bowls from where Zeke had put them, on the top shelf of the dishwasher, down to the bottom, where they fit better.

"Casey?"

"He heard you, Ibbit," Zeke said.

"All right, then. Pop and I will meet you at the cages. And, Casey, make sure you call your mother today."

We walked out to the gym, where I grabbed a handful of trash bags from the supply closet.

"Why's your dad all over you about your mom?" Zeke asked.

I shrugged.

"You been talking to her more?"

I shook my head.

"Hmm," he said, as though he sensed deep meaning.

Screwball

LONG before I was born, back when Pop was an umpire for Major League Baseball, the grounds that now belonged to Behind the Plate were used by a reform school. I didn't think they still had reform schools exactly. Dad said they probably called them something different now, like Attitude Improvement Academies or Boarding Schools for Pre-Criminals, but back then, this was where the bad boys of New Jersey — too young for prison — had been sent.

Reform-school students attended classes here and were also expected to maintain the grounds. Which could have made me feel like a reform-school kid. I did a lot of chores at BTP — checking inventory, ordering supplies, inspecting the dorms. It was expected of me, the same way a farm kid would know it was his job to milk the cows. Except ... I wondered if farm kids minded doing their chores. Because I never did.

Zeke, of course, didn't *have* to do anything—but he loved this place as much as I did and spent nearly as much time here as I did. We only spent time at his house when we had to study for a big test or get school projects done—because there was nothing there that could distract us. Like, nothing. His parents were always at work, and their house was just . . . boring. They didn't have any video games, no pets. There weren't even any chores for us to do there. (Not that I was complaining about that.)

There was always something to do, or watch, at BTP. Zeke once got to chalk the fields for a month, the year Pop had knee replacement surgery. It was the highlight of his life.

The only thing Zeke liked as much as being part of BTP was watching reality TV. Stupid animal tricks, brainless gross-out challenges, talent show performances, all the garbage you could never pay me to watch—Zeke never missed it. He wanted nothing more than to be on one of those shows.

He said it would be his claim to fame. Breaking into reality TV.

The claim to fame I wanted was more serious: I wanted to write award-winning newspaper articles. It was weird—I didn't know what they would be about. In fact, the only thing I could see was my byline—*by Casey Snowden.*

I pushed open the door to the batting cages. The building used to be a garage for whatever kinds of vehicles they housed at reform schools, but it always looked more like a stable to me. There were five batting cages here, divided by netting and some kind of plasticky tarp. Each cage had a pitching machine and home plate/backstop set up and an Ibbit stick, the contraption Dad, aka Ibbit, invented to show students how to line up their feet when in the crouch behind the plate. (If you didn't know what it was, you might wonder why someone would nail rulers and yardsticks together at weird angles.) Students came out here in groups of five every day to work on the mechanics of making calls behind the plate. Most students came to Academy with some umpiring experience—Little League, rec leagues, travel baseball, sometimes college ball. They knew the basics, but at BTP, we taught the exact-right way to umpire a game.

Zeke was examining a video camera. "Can you give me one of those memory cards?" he asked, pointing at the little box where we kept all the camera stuff.

I handed him one. "We forgot the first-aid kits," I said. "I'll check on those. Be right back."

I walked through the gym back to the first class-room, where the desks were already in neat rows. I finally found Dad and Bobbybo unstacking desks in the classroom at the end of the hall. Pop was supervising.

"Do you need the first-aid kits restocked?"

"It's on the master list, isn't it?" Pop said.

"We probably won't need them right away," Dad said.

"Famous last words," Pop said.

"Well, we don't do much fieldwork at first, so no opportunity for anyone to get hurt."

"Then watch a student get stabbed with a pencil in the first hour here. It's never a mistake to be ready for everything."

Bobbybo smiled at me, and I knew why—Pop always spoke in life lessons, and I bet he'd missed Pop, and Dad, and everything. I was sure Behind the Plate was a hard place to be away from. Luckily, I never had to find out for myself.

"Just tell Mrs. G. you're taking care of it," Dad said. "So she can mark it off the list."

"Will do," I said.

I crossed the hallway to the office. Mrs. G. was sitting with her granddaughter.

"Hi, Sly," I said. For some reason, my voice sounded like I was talking to a baby. She scowled at me.

"Baby, you know my daughter, Dana, right?" Mrs. G. said.

I'd heard of her. I nodded.

"She's been taking on some extra jobs — you know how that goes. She'll be coming to pick up Sylvia later."

Mrs. G. talked to me sometimes like I was fifty or something. "Sure, sure," I said. Because I couldn't really say, "Mrs. G., I'm twelve. What do you think I really know about extra jobs and little kids?" Not to mention mothers.

She was still talking. "Anyway, Dana's sitter quit, so I have Sylvia with me here today. Is there anything she can do to help you boys get ready?"

"Sly!" the girl said. "No one calls me Sylvia, Grandma."

"I don't think so, thanks. I was just getting the first-aid —"

"That is *exactly* the kind of thing Sylvia can do. Get the kits — they're in the clos — Oh, why am I telling you? Sylvia, this boy could run this whole school by himself if he had to."

I didn't really think I could run the school, but I did know a lot.

I pulled the first-aid boxes from the supply closet, then climbed to the top shelf and pushed aside random spare parts from leg guards, helmets, and chest protectors (the Snowdens were of the you-never-know-when-you-might-need-this school of never throwing anything away) until I found the checklist of all the things that needed to be in each kit.

I showed Sly the list and explained that she needed to open every kit, check the expiration dates, count out bandages, and make sure everything on the list was in the box.

"Hey, what if a bandage is kind of gross, like this one?" She held one up that was half opened and nasty looking.

"Then you throw it out."

"Could I keep it?"

The kid was creepy. "I guess," I said.

"Cool."

By the time I got back to the batting cages, Zeke had finished checking all the cameras. He was holding one and playing with its buttons.

"Does your dad know this one's broken?" he asked.

"What's wrong with it?"

"This thing doesn't stay closed, so you have to keep your hand on it. It's no big deal or anything, as long as whoever's using this camera knows about it."

Dad and Pop joined us then, and Zeke showed them the sort-of-broken camera.

"So how many are working?" Dad asked.

"The other four are fine. And this one still works. You just have to hold it shut."

"You never want to make it easy for someone to screw up," Pop said.

"We have what," Dad said, "eighty students? Four cameras'll be enough. But let's replace that one so we're ready for next year."

"You can probably get it fixed, right?" Zeke said.

"It's usually as much to fix it as it is to replace it, and that's a pretty old one," Dad said.

Wait, what? Did Dad say eighty? That had to be wrong. There were always at least a hundred students for Academy.

"I have this idea," Zeke said before I could ask. I managed not to groan.

Dad said, "Let me guess: You want to keep the camera."

"No," Zeke said. "I mean, that wasn't my idea. But wow, yeah. Sick! I do." He looked at me. "But wouldn't you want it?" he asked.

Sly walked in with two first-aid kits. "Where do I put these?" she asked me.

"Why's the kid here?" Zeke asked.

Pop fake-slapped Zeke's head with his open hand. "Don't be rude. This is Mrs. G.'s granddaughter, Sylvia."

"Sly," she said with a sigh.

"So I had this IDEA," Zeke said again. "Have you ever thought of shooting before-and-after videos of each student?"

"We film them every day," Pop said. "In the cages."

"No," Zeke said, "I mean if I get each student out on the field, doing calls behind the plate the first few days and then again at the end of the session. The cage tapes are so gradual, but if you showed a real before-and-after tape —"

"Excuse me," Sly said. "Where are the cages?"

"These are the cages, sweetheart," Pop said, motioning to the whole building.

"You lock people in there or animals?"

"No," I said. "No one gets locked in. They're called batting cages."

"So they practice batting hits in there?"

"Where's Mrs. G.?" Pop said, his patience suddenly evaporated. "Let me take you back to the office."

"Thanks for bringing out the first-aid kits," Dad said. Then he turned to Zeke and said, "I like the idea, but you can't do all that camera work. I'll put some staff on it too. It's a good idea. You can help out after school."

Even I had to admit it — it was good. The students

all improved so much, and seeing it like that, on video, would be really sweet.

Zeke was still beaming as we headed back outside. "About that camera," he said. "Your dad should have offered it to you first. I mean, he's YOUR dad."

"He knows I wouldn't use it," I said. The thought of going out and filming stuff did seem pretty cool, but I knew I'd never really do it. There was this big box of stuff, unused stuff, in my room: lacrosse stick, bowling ball in a rolling case, microscope. I knew the camera would just get added to it.

But I did have a quick and bad thought about how we might actually be helping Zeke achieve his stupid goal of getting something on TV by putting a camera in his hand. It was as though I could see this huge banner headline: BREAKING NEWS: GUESS WHO GAVE REALITY TV'S ZEKE THE FREAK THE CAMERA?

Teammates

ZEKE and I were sitting in the center of the gym, surrounded by a sea of registration papers. I looked a second time at the form in my hand. "I didn't know there was a woman this year," I said. "June Sponato."

"I love the lady umpires!"

Zeke really did. Every few years, a woman signed up, but none of them had been very . . . girlie. Students all wore the same gray-pants-blue-shirt-and-hat uniform, and the women pretty much blended in. Zeke always held out hope that some contestant from *America's Next Top Model* was going to sign up at BTP.

"So no roommate, right?"

"Not unless there's another woman," I said. "Put her on the third floor. She'll get that extra bathroom all to herself."

This was the absolute highlight of getting ready for Academy. We were checking the list over to catch things a computer might miss, like making sure no woman had been assigned to room with a man. But really, what we were hoping to discover was the next great roommate name matchup. Dad's umpire-school roommate had been Joseph Costello. Everyone called them Abbott and Costello, and somehow—this is the part I always wondered about, but Dad said he had no idea how it happened—Abbott turned into Ibbit, which is what everyone but Pop and I called him now.

I loved this part, the name part. I guess there was a pretty good reason for it—my own stupid name. The way the story goes: my parents could not agree on a name, even after I was born. For days, the names my dad liked—Jeter, Gehrig, Robinson—were all just too much baseball for my mother. Finally, still unable to agree when I was almost a week old, she asked Dad, "Wasn't there a poem or something about a baseball player named Casey? Could we maybe compromise and go with that?"

She was right. There was. A very famous poem. But somehow, neither one of them thought about the fact that they were naming me for a fictional guy famous for striking out. I guess it's better than naming me after Babe Ruth—a pig's name AND a girl's name. So I've got that going for me.

Zeke was running down the student list with his index finger, and he stopped at room 208. "We've got a Bob Franklin and a Robbie Franklin, one from Delaware and one from West Orange. What's the call?"

"Same last name, probably both Robert, but different nicknames. Let's come back to that."

"Okey dokey," Zeke said. "Oh, look at this. "Didn't we have a whole group of Mcs and Macs last year too?" Zeke asked. He read their names out loud: "MacGregor, Mackenzie, MacNamara, MacSophal, McDonaldson."

"I think that was the year before," I said. "Did we end up breaking those pairs up into different rooms? No, wait. No! We realized later that we should have, because they all called each other *Mac*, remember?"

"But then they started with Big Mac and Fat Mac and Forehead Mac, right? You know I'm a fan of the creative nicknames."

"Yeah. But let's break those all up this year."

Zeke was staring at the printout. "MacSophal," he said. "Remember that name?"

"Yeah, you just said it."

"Come on. Stay with me, Snowden. MacSophal. Remember J-Mac?"

"That relief pitcher with the Phillies? The steroid guy with the crazy beard?"

"Jimmy *MacSophal*," he said.

I reached for the dorm roommate form. "This guy's name's Patrick."

"Oh," Zeke said. "Different guy."

"What," I said laughing, "you thought some former major leaguer was going to attend BTP?"

Zeke shrugged. We got back to work.

I heard a little girl's voice ask "What are you doing?" I hadn't even heard the door open.

Zeke whispered, "No. Make her go away."

Pop once told me that if you see a stray dog, you don't make eye contact. You remain calm, and you pretend it's not there. You never look its way. That was my plan. And, apparently, Zeke's too. It was one of those unspoken things between friends.

Even though I was busy very much not watching Mrs. G.'s granddaughter, I could sort of *feel* her . . . walking around us. Like she was studying us or something. I wasn't even sure I knew what the word meant, but I had the feeling she was *skulking*.

"So back to the Franklins," Zeke said. "The call is Robbie/Bob, too close or different enough to be roommates without confusion?"

"I could go for Robbie/Bob under normal circumstances," I said, still not looking at the girl. "But in this case, we have the same last name. So many guys go by their last names, right? Like remember Mankowitz? Hey, Mankowitz!"

Stan Mankowitz was the shortest student in BTP history. I had no idea who suggested umpiring as a possible profession to him, but that person steered him wrong. You need to be able to see over the catcher. Dad and Pop tried everything, using phone books and stools for him to stand on, but he dropped out after the first two weeks.

Mankowitz!

"What're all these papers?" Sly asked.

"Your name is Sylvia, right?" Zeke said.

"Sly."

"Don't you have some other place to be?" Zeke asked. His voice was a little nasty, but Sly didn't know him well enough to notice.

She shook her head.

To Zeke, I said, "Split up the Franklins."

"Got it, chief."

Sly either hadn't noticed that we were ignoring her or didn't care. "So this is where you teach the baseball?"

I didn't even know where to start. I didn't want to start. Zeke and I waited all year for this, and yeah, it was true that we loved it way more than two guys our age should have, but there was just no room for an annoying little kid here right now.

"Can I help?" Sly asked.

"Not really," I said, still not making eye contact. "Maybe you could ask your grandmother if there's anything else on the master list you could do. Me and Zeke got this covered."

"She sent me out to ask you."

"Well, like he said," Zeke said, "we're good. Tell your grandma we said thanks."

I knew he thought that would send her scampering back to Mrs. G., but this girl clearly wanted to hang with Zeke. And me.

"That's okay. I'll just stay here with you guys and help."

"Oh, you know what she should do?" Zeke said.

"What might that be, Ezekiel?"

"Room fresheners!"

I loved that guy. Seriously, sometimes he just pulled one out.

LEMON-SCENTED HAIL-MARY PLAY SAVES DAY.

I told Sly to ask her grandmother where to find the

plug-in room deodorizers and to put one in each dorm room and one in each bathroom outlet. Umpire-school students, for some reason, tended to be on the stinky side.

Zeke and I high-fived each other all over the place when she left and moved through the list a little faster than we might have otherwise, knowing we were on limited time. Everything went well, but there was no great roommate name pair to be found this year. We ended up with one guy in a single room—June Sponato had thrown off the even matchups.

We went to the dorm and worked our way down the hall, starting on the first floor. The carpet was getting kind of rundown here, and there was this old-building smell. I didn't think it was mold, but it had something to do with moisture or humidity or something. That was just how it was—old boarding schools don't smell great. Maybe the room fresheners would help.

We started to hang names on the doors—all doubles, except for a single name on June's room and one on the door for Jorge Washington. It reminded me of the time a few years ago when Zeke tried hanging his own name on one of the doors. But he never needed to do that. It was just a fact that he practically lived here for the whole Academy. His parents didn't expect him to even check in with them — they knew where to find him.

We finished hanging all the names. But it seemed like way too many rooms were empty. Were there really just eighty students this year?

Cut from the Team

OUR house used to be the headmaster's house, back in its reform-school days, and there was a certain old weirdness to it that I really loved. There were a lot of little rooms, and we used many of them in ways that probably were not intended whenever this house was built. Like one room that was probably supposed to be the dining room was stuffed with dirty old equipment bags filled with baseballs, gloves, catching gear, and old bases. Another had the furniture from Pop's house, from back when Grandma was still alive, when I was just a baby. It was a dark room with dark wood furniture, really heavy, sitting up against the walls, some of it covered with cloth. A lot of framed photos that used to be all over the house were now in that room, too, mostly wedding pictures of my parents.

There was one of Dad and Pop on the day my parents got married. Pop was taller than Dad then. And now he was shorter. (They were briefly the same height again after Pop's double knee replacement surgery. Apparently new knees make you taller.) And there was one of my dad — at least they told me it was my dad — when he was about my age. My mother, or Mrs. Bob the Baker, as I called her, always loved that picture. The weirdest thing was that how he looked then, in that picture, looked just like me now, except his hair was darker and shorter. Mine was on the brown side of blond, and his was more straight-up brown. But everything else — the sort of long shape of the face, skinny kid body, even the way he was standing — seemed just like me. I kept meaning to bring that picture to my room.

When my mother left, we closed off the whole third floor. Three guys just didn't need that much house. All that used to be up there was her office and a room she called the craft room but hardly ever used, a bathroom with a leaky tub, and a guest room that we didn't need because the only guests who came were students, and they stayed in the dorms. A long time ago, Pop lived up on the third floor too, but as his body parts started giving out, he moved down to the second floor, near my room and Dad's.

The one room that got a lot of use at our house

was the kitchen. At dinnertime. Zeke and I joined Dad and Pop there for our annual day-before pizza. Like always, Dad had sent staff to have dinner in town at the Well.

I sometimes checked on Pop for signs of wear. That was a term Mrs. G. used when she inspected old classroom equipment. Every year when Academy rolled around, I looked at Pop to see if he seemed like he was getting really old. But he was like one of those old-school baseball managers who look the same every year. Maybe it was the baseball cap he always wore, but I bet it was more than just that. Those old-time managers, usually ones who played ball before managing, have these smart-seeming eyes, eyes that have seen a lot of ball. Pop's eyes were like that. When Pop watched students, his eyes often had something like fire in them. But when he looked at me, there was this really obvious . . . love.

There were probably more wrinkles near his eyes and mouth than there used to be, but that was okay. He still looked like Pop, and he hadn't needed a new body part in a couple of years. That was pretty good.

"'Isisooogood," Zeke said, a slice of pizza in his mouth.

I accidentally looked in his direction; he was a truly disgusting eater. There was food where there shouldn't be food, and the combination of chewed-up pizza and his very metallic mouth was not one of my all-time favorite sights. I never knew if it was because of the double-dentist-parent thing or what, but he had more braces than you'd ever seen in a mouth.

Dad put a slice on his plate. "I'm just going to say this," he said. "I had to call a couple of guys and tell them not to come this year. Phillip Masterson, Steamboat, and To-Go. We don't have enough students for me to pay everyone."

Wait, WHAT? This is what they were not talking about in front of me? But. But. But. This never happened. I wanted to plug my ears with my fingers and hum so I didn't have to hear this.

I loved Steamboat. When I was little, he gave me a rookie baseball card of my favorite player, Jackson Alter. I still have it. And I think I'm the only person who knows Steamboat's real name: Kelly. He told me because he said we shared a girls'-names bond. So no Steamboat? I couldn't even find words. I guess no one could, because we ate the rest of the meal in silence.

Finally, Dad asked, "Are we remembering everything?"

Pop nodded, slow and steady as a rocking chair.

It was the same every year. Dad wondered if he was forgetting something. He always worried, but he never really forgot. They used the same master list every year. The same worksheets and homework and tests for the students. The same everything.

"Baseball doesn't change, so we don't need to change," Pop always said.

That always used to feel true. But we'd never had to cut back on staff before.

✱✱✱

Right after Zeke went home, I realized I'd been meaning to ask if I could go with him and his mom to get school supplies. I tried his cell, but I knew no one would answer. I didn't even know why he had it, other than his parents claiming they wanted to be able to call him at any time (even if they never actually did). Dad and Pop would be meeting with staff until too late, after Paper Depot closed. Our BTP store had lots of supplies but not all the right kinds. (If I had needed a ball and strike indicator for any of my middle-school classes, I'd have been in business.) My teachers wanted all kinds of notebooks and folders and stuff, and we had to have everything by tomorrow.

There was this sign that hung in the gym. It said SURPRISE IS THE ENEMY OF THE UMPIRE, and it was true. Like any good umpire, I did not like to be caught off-guard. By anything. And yet as I tried to figure out a way to get to Paper Depot, I got caught off-guard by a memory. A memory! I was suddenly thinking about the last time Mrs. Bob the Baker packed my backpack, in third grade: I could still see a row of perfectly sharpened pencils in a brand-new pencil case.

I started to think about how long it had been since then, but before a whole mess of feelings started pouring down, I turned them off.

And I asked Mrs. G. if she could drive me to Paper Depot.

Mrs. G. was always able to bail me out when there was no parent around to help. But instead of smiling and grabbing her keys, she winced, like maybe she'd bitten the inside of her cheek.

"Baby, Dana picked up Sly, but now she needs me to get home and watch her. You know I'd never say no to you if I had—"

"That's okay. Do you think you could maybe drop me at the store and I'll—"

"What? Walk home by yourself? I don't like the sound of that. No, sir. Here's what we're going to do. I'll swing by to pick up Sly and take her with us. Then I'll drop you home afterward."

I knew that after a long day she'd probably rather just go home, but I really did need to get notebooks and a ruler and protractor and compass. And about a thousand other things. She reached into her bun — this is true — and pulled out her car key. "Let's go, Baby."

✳ ✳ ✳

It didn't take long for me to regret asking Mrs. G. From the minute she climbed into the back seat, Sly pelted me with questions about lunch boxes and spiral notebooks and in what grade you get to start using pens, because she was getting pretty sick of pencils, and did I ever see the *SpongeBob* episode where Squidward turns the adults into babies. Seriously, I thought my head was going to burst.

I had lived among men for a long time. Men knew that quiet was fine. Quiet could be good.

I walked up and down all the aisles and finally filled the cart with everything I needed. Sly insisted on helping me unload the cart at the cash register. But when the time came to hand over my money, I was embarrassed. Really embarrassed. I'd forgotten to bring any!

"Not to worry, Baby," Mrs. G. said, pulling out a credit card (from her wallet, not her hair). "I know where you live."

I thanked Mrs. G. as the cashier put all my stuff into plastic bags.

When we pulled up in front of my house, Mrs. G. helped me get the bags from her trunk and then put her hand up like a traffic cop's. "Do NOT thank me again, Baby. I was happy to do it."

"Okay," I said. "Thanks."

✳✳✳

I sat at the kitchen table, trying to force my giant science textbook into a green book sock. When Dad and Pop walked in, Pop said, "Oh, that's right, Casey. How was today? How was school?"

"School?" Dad said. He looked at me, at all the school supplies I was labeling and wrestling and organizing, as though he hadn't seen them in front of him until then. "Right. First day of middle school. So where'd all this come from?"

"Mrs. G. took me to the store. I needed some stuff."

He got this look. It was kind of complicated.

Most years we had this really awkward talk right about now. It was basically him saying that he was sorry in advance for not being around the way he usually was, for how Academy took nearly all his time. Last year I begged him to stop having that talk, told him I was old enough and I understood. But still, there was something in his look tonight that was maybe a little different, had something to do with my mother, and that got me thinking about how she used to sit at this table with me and cover my books for me and neatly label the dividers I put in my binders. I didn't know if Dad was thinking I should have a mother here to help me with things like that or if he was feeling bad that he hadn't talked to me at all, really, about this sort of important thing — me starting middle school — or if it was more him missing my mother, and that was one of those things I didn't like to think about. It was like I turned into Sly or something: I just started talking.

"I needed these book covers for all my books, and a different binder for each subject, but I don't know how you're supposed to fit four binders and a notebook and everything else into your backpack, because I have to bring them all to school tomorrow, and I have no idea how I should do that. And also what I bought in the cafeteria today was disgusting, and I'm not even sure that was really ham, and Mrs. G. paid for everything at Paper Depot, so we have to pay her —"

"Did you ever call your mother?" Dad said.

Foul! That's a foul! That ball is way out of bounds!

Why didn't he know that bringing her up was outside the lines of fair play?

"I didn't have time," I said, no longer interested in talking.

"Don't you think your mother might want to hear how your first day of middle school went? I'm sure there are two or three messages from her."

I just didn't get the why of this. Why now? We could go months without talking, but when I started a new school, it suddenly became the most important thing in her life?

"Casey, I know you're hurt, or angry, or both. I really do get that." I looked at him then and could tell that, no, he really didn't get it.

"You don't need to talk long, but she needs to hear from you."

I still didn't say anything.

My dad shook his head. His look said he was disgusted with me. Or maybe ashamed of me. "And you need a haircut, Casey," he said.

"So do you, Dad." Somehow, that took the mad right out of him. When he took off his baseball cap at the end of the day, he had horrible hat hair, squished down, and it made him look . . . sad.

Like groceries, scheduling haircuts was something we couldn't really get the hang of. Sometimes it wasn't only my name that got me mistaken for a girl—my hair really was too long. So was Dad's. If Pop had had hair, I bet his would have been too long, too.

Dad was still shaking his too-long-haired head when he went upstairs to bed.

✳✳✳

A long time ago, I fell on my knee when I was climbing the fence behind the rear field's first-base dugout. I probably needed stitches, but I didn't want to tell my dad, because I'm not supposed to climb on school property. As any self-respecting kid could tell you, if you break the rules and nobody finds out, you don't get in trouble. It was kind of hard to admit I'd done something wrong when I knew I might be able to get away with it. So I just took care of it myself with one of the first-aid kits. I never told anyone.

But the stupid cut kept opening. And each time, it hurt like a whole new injury.

That's what I was reminded of every time Dad talked about Mrs. Bob the Baker. The way that even when you think something has healed, it can keep opening, all raw and red, and hurt you over and over again.

Old-School Rivalry

AS I was leaving the next morning, I took a quick look around.

By the time the school day was over, my quiet home would have again been invaded. There would be eighty guys here I'd never seen before. They would have met all the instructors, toured the campus, learning which field was which and where the lecture hall, cafeteria, and classrooms were, the batting cages, all of it. They'd have gotten set up in their rooms with their roommates—except, of course, for June Sponato and Jorge Washington.

I tried to memorize how clean it all looked, because the ground would soon be littered with spit-out sunflower seeds, ground-out cigarettes, and random pieces of trash. This used to be Mrs. Bob the Baker's least favorite day—she said it was a form of torture watching her quiet home turn into a college campus for dumb athletes overnight. She never really got it.

Dad and Pop did more classroom teaching and less fieldwork the first two days as they waited for all the staff to arrive. Some instructors straggled in late because the minor league baseball season had just ended. The ones who'd been umping road games had to get home to pull their stuff together before heading to Clay Coves.

Umpire Academy was the first step toward becoming a major league umpire. Three of Dad's graduates had made it to the majors already. In a way, that seemed like something to be really proud of. But BTP was one of only three umpire schools in the country. And most people would agree it was considered the third best. Still, it was the only place I ever wanted to be.

✳✳✳

Middle school was supposed to be this big-deal change from elementary school, but it was pretty much the way I'd imagined it. Subject classes were just as boring as everything had been in fifth grade, except now we got to move from room to room instead of just being bored in the same classroom all day. I had lunch the same period as Zeke, which was good. And it was great to hang out with some of the guys I hadn't seen much over the summer—Charley Haddon, Franco Spinelli, Andrew deFausto.

Day two of school was going fine until I ran into this older kid, Chris Sykes, in the hall. "Snowden," he said, with something that was probably pure hatred sticking in his voice.

"How you doing, Chris?" I said. I put my Sly-Avoidance Technique into place and continued down the hall to the auditorium, where there was some assembly for new students.

I didn't see Chris Sykes often, but when I did, he always pointed me out to his friends and whispered something. He was a great athlete, and he had one of those fathers—there were a lot in our town—who thought they knew everything about every sport.

The reason Chris Sykes hated me had to do with a call my dad made. It wasn't even a call on the field. Dad used to volunteer as an ump for Little League in our town, until the parents, like Chris's dad, made him so crazy he stopped. It was the same year I stopped playing. But this one year, Dad was overseeing the umps in a big statewide baseball tournament. I guess Chris had always played with older kids—he was that good—but the tournament rules very clearly said that you had to be a certain age to play. Chris's coach pretended he hadn't known that, wouldn't show Dad Chris's birth certificate, and everyone was furious with Dad when he said Chris couldn't play.

Chris had been a jerk to me ever since.

Did Chris Sykes think I had something to do with my dad enforcing rules? We were on the same bus route then, going to Clay Coves Elementary. And he told everyone that my dad ran a vampire school. He got all his friends to open their mouths really wide and hiss whenever I walked down the aisle of the bus.

It didn't last long, though. Maybe because I thought it was pretty funny. Or funny for something that was supposed to be mean, at least. Right? Tell me you can't picture a vampire school! There would be classes like How to Avoid Mirrors, and Perfecting Neck Angle, and Fang Care. I loved picturing the fieldwork (at night, of course) — all those guys out there on the same field we used, except instead of wearing their umpire shirt and pants, they'd all be in black capes, learning how to swirl them in a sort of villainy vampire way in the dark of night. For a mean kid who was trying to annoy me, he had come up with a pretty funny idea.

At the assembly, I couldn't find Zeke, so I sat with this kid I sort of knew, Juan. He took notes about everything. Even things like when the girls' soccer tryouts were. I wondered if he thought there were tests on assemblies. I wondered if maybe there were.

When someone walked onstage to read a list of all the different nonsport school activities and clubs, I almost let out a loud WOO HOOO! at the mention of the school newspaper.

I had big stacks of filled-up notebooks on the shelves in my room. When I watched games on TV, I wrote down the great plays. I tried to write them in as interesting a way as I could, not just describing what happened, but also using words that let the reader feel the same excitement I did, or any fan did, watching the play actually take place. I didn't know if the middle-school newspaper had a sports section. If it didn't, maybe I could start one, reporting on the different school teams. Or maybe I could write *and* be the sports editor.

So okay, then, maybe I *should* have written down when the girls' soccer tryouts were too. Maybe Juan was a little sharper than I thought.

Play Ball

ON the bus home, Zeke talked about last night's episode of *So You Think You're the Biggest Idiot?* "There was this one guy, right? He was jumping on a trampoline, but of course he didn't know anyone was filming him? So he started taking off his clothes. I mean, they couldn't show anything, they had this blurry thing going on the screen, so you couldn't see, but there were people — his neighbors, I think — who came out and were watching him? And they were describing what they saw, and he didn't know they were there. And it was, like, one of the funniest things I ever saw in my entire life. It was sick!"

"Sounds like it," I said. I never saw the point of wanting the title of Biggest Idiot.

"Are you going to watch tonight?"

Zeke still couldn't accept that I just wasn't into those shows. There was one time when he swore I would love this new show, and from the title, I thought he might be right, so I decided to give it a try. I watched the first-ever season of *Reporter Standoff*. Contestants had eighteen hours to find, research, and write a different kind of story each week. Sometimes it was for a newspaper, sometimes radio, or broadcast TV. I loved it! There was this guy, Feury—I had wanted him to win so bad. (Tell me that isn't the greatest name ever!) I had cheered for him. I loved how his cool little brother held up signs for him: RAGING FEURY! But then, poof, Feury was voted off. You got all attached, you counted on seeing this guy week after week, and then he was off the show. Gone.

Big surprise—all I really watched was sports and ESPN. You could count on sports. No matter what happened in a game, you would start at the same point next time. A clean court, a newly chalked field, a Zambonied rink. A new story every time.

*** *** ***

After school, we got off the bus and turned the corner, and as we walked through the gate and down the long driveway, we could see that the parking lot was almost full. There were license plates from Massachusetts, Connecticut, New York, Virginia, Maryland, D.C.

There was no one outside, so we must have missed afternoon break.

We dropped our backpacks in the house and headed over to the main building. Mrs. G. looked a little frazzled. The first day was always hard.

"How's it going, Mrs. G.?" I asked.

"Do you know where your father keeps the liquor?" she said. Then she barked her hard, loud laugh.

Zeke cracked up, but I always worried that maybe Mrs. G. was stepping a little bit over the line onto the crazy side. And I preferred normalcy and peace in my life. I loved peace.

"Aspirin, maybe?" I offered.

"I'm just kidding you, Baby. It hasn't been too bad. We're managing. Chet was late with lunch, but they got it served, so your father didn't kill me or anything. Oh, Chet left your lunch for tomorrow here," she said, pointing to a brown bag. That was the best part of Umpire Academy — my lunches were made for me by Chet. The rest of the year, I just bought lunch at school, but after the gross not-sure-that-was-really-ham sandwich and not-quite-chicken nuggets I'd had so far, I was extra happy to have Chet around for the next five weeks.

Zeke, the ever-hungry, started to reach for the bag, and I swatted his hand away.

"Chet should really make me lunch too. Could he do that?" Zeke asked.

"So I could carry two lunches to school?" I said. "Anyway, it would remove the comedy from my life. Your lunches are always one of the highlights of my day."

Zeke's parents stopped making his lunches when Zeke was in third grade, when they found that he kept trading away what they gave him for fruit roll-ups. He would trade anything — sometimes his whole lunch — for fruit roll-ups. Which he wasn't supposed to eat. Because of his braces. Ever since then, he had just . . . had a very creative approach to what belonged in a lunch bag.

We were about to head out to the lecture hall when Mrs. G. said, "Oh, I almost forgot. One new student showed up this morning."

"Do you have the papers?" I asked. "Is he all set?"

"We put him in that room with Jorge Washington," she said. "That student with no roommate. I took care of the papers."

"Great," I said. "What's his name?"

"Cabrera," she said. "Hang on a second." She quickly looked through a pile and pulled out a form. "Lincoln Cabrera."

I was back outside before it hit me. "Did you hear that?" I asked.

Zeke looked at me like, *Hear what?* before it registered for him, too. "Jorge Washington's new roommate is named Lincoln?"

We high-fived. "Roommate pair of the year."

"Quite possibly of all time," I said. "All hail Jorge Washington and Lincoln Cabrera!"

"And their presidential suite!"

"Sweet!" I said.

✱✱✱

We walked to the lecture hall. Dad and Pop were at the front, rows of students with notebooks looking up at them. Pop, in the grungy green baseball cap he always wore through all five weeks of Academy, was sitting on a stool looking out at the students, and Dad was talking, pacing back and forth at the front of the room. There was something about my dad, something hard to name, that screamed *teacher*. It might have been the way he'd stop pacing and roll back on his heels. That always seemed like a teacher thing to me. I happened to know this was his secret way of stretching his hamstrings. Or something like that. But it really did make him look like someone in charge.

When you looked at umpires at a major league game, so many of them seemed to be big, overweight guys. But they didn't leave umpire school looking that way — most students were in their twenties, and BTP had had guys as young as eighteen. (And we once had a sixty-eight-year-old guy from Canada.)

Seeing major league players in person was always surprising. They looked bigger than they did on TV, like supersized humans. Umpire-school students looked more like the way you'd expect a baseball player to look, without the supersizing.

Dad was going over the necessity of wearing a cup at all times. I scanned the seats for June Sponato, and before I found her, Zeke poked me in the stomach with his elbow and pointed at her. As predicted, she was not a supermodel. I glanced at Zeke, but he didn't look disappointed. In fact, he was beaming. He lived for this. We both did. (You probably got that already. And if not, hello? Is everything okay over there?)

Dad was near the end of his lesson. "We've gone over some of the most basic rules and interpretations of the rules. We'll be doing that through the whole five weeks. And just so everyone understands the process from day one, here's how our Umpire Academy works. At the end of five weeks of intense education, training, and drills, we will select the top students based on your performance here in the classroom and, even more so, out on the field. Up to ten of you will have the opportunity to attend the Professional Baseball Umpire Corp. Evaluation Course for minor league umpires in Cocoa, Florida, next March. As you know, that's pretty much where you audition to be selected as minor league umpires. From there, you can work your way up to the major leagues. But you can't get there if you don't do your work here."

I looked around the room for familiar faces. Sometimes students who didn't make it to PBUC came back for another try. No one in this group looked familiar to me, though.

"We're going to finish up in here, then head to the field for some stretches and drills," he said. "When you've finished your drills, I want Groups A and B to report to field one for filming. Everybody turn around and wave to my son, Casey, and his friend Zeke back there in the last row."

There was a loud rustle as heads turned around to look at us. People nodded or smiled or put up a hand to say hi. Some had smirks on their faces, like, *Look! Little kids!* Probably the same way Zeke and I looked when Sly came into the gym yesterday.

"Those boys are two of the hardest workers you're ever going to want to meet."

I knew I was turning colors that were more natural in fruit and flowers than they were in human persons. I liked what he was saying—kind of loved it—but it hurt my face when this much blood went there.

"They are going to film your technique beginning this afternoon," Dad said. "You will not be judged on your performance today, as we understand that some of you have more experience than others. Each of you will leave here with, in addition to your filmed batting cage work, a before-and-after video. I don't mean to sound like an infomercial here, boys. Boys and June, that is. But I stand up here today to guarantee that even those of you coming here with years of experience will see a huge difference in the work you do, in your body language, your confidence, your authority, your stance, your posture, your command of the game. Even those of you not selected to go to Cocoa will leave here better umpires. Okay, let's hustle out to the gym."

Dad stood there, rolling back on his heels.

I watched as the class stood. It was an every-man-and-June-by-and-for-him/herself kind of scene. As the days went on, they'd break up into groups and cliques. Right now they seemed a little nervous, a little like, say, middle-school students. Within days, they'd learn how much Dad and Pop liked to see hustle. They'd be jogging between stations, standing straight, looking their instructors in the eye when they talked to them. Everyone wanted that shot at being a professional umpire.

Mrs. Bob the Baker always complained that everything at BTP seemed so *military*. She said that word as though it were something negative.

But that was one of the things I'd always loved best about BTP. The order. By late tomorrow, students would know how to stand in formation on the field, Group A two feet off the right-field foul line, and all the groups back from there, spread out at exact and even intervals. They'd learn the basic mechanics of calling balls and strikes, safe and out, foul balls and balks. They'd run through the drills, doing the exact same moves at the exact same time, like they were one person.

But not yet. Now they were this big globby mob, all trying to fit through one narrow doorway at once.

Zeke was still sitting there, grinning like some kind of learning-impaired monkey.

"What?"

"Did you hear what he said?"

I knew Zeke was talking about the videos, but I couldn't resist. "Oh, don't worry. *You* don't need to wear a cup. He meant the students. It's in case they get hit. With a ball. In that spot. Where it hurts."

He slapped my head the same way Pop sometimes did.

"I'm really doing the filming."

Televised Game

ZEKE spent two hours filming. I worked as his assistant, organizing and labeling, running students through the different calls, making careful notes about the order, so that the before videos would match the afters.

Once we got through Groups A and B, Zeke went home.

Sometimes the first day ran really long. Most BTP school days were eight to five thirty, followed by dinner in the cafeteria. Dad and Pop had dinner with me most nights, but on the first day of school, they liked to be available to students, because they were usually falling all over each other with questions.

I finished my homework and turned on the game. Jackson Alter was trying to extend a twenty-four-game hitting streak, and there was no way I was going to miss that. If anyone was ever going to beat DiMaggio's fifty-six-game streak, he was the one my money was on. I watched, scribbling in my notebook.

Dad and Pop watched games on TV like umpires. They saw which crew was calling the game and said things like "Oh, at least it'll be a quick one" or "You know a manager's going to be thrown out tonight." It made sense: Both Dad and Pop had worked as umpires. Dad made it to the minor leagues before he and Pop opened up BTP.

For me, though, it wasn't about the umpires. There was time within a baseball game — lots of time — but unlike most other sports, no clock. The game had a rhythm, a slow one, familiar. It was the kind of sport that let your brain drift a little, almost, to find the connections, the surprises, the stories.

I didn't even have a favorite team, unless it was whatever team Jackson Alter was playing for. He started as a backup utility infielder for the Yankees. And then, even though he was an amazing shortstop, he got traded a lot. He went from the Yankees to the Cubs to the Phillies to the Cardinals, and for the past year, he'd been on the Orioles. Wherever he was, I loved watching him play. He was fast and crisp, and he seemed like a really good guy.

I loved the way Jackson tried to make plays that

seemed impossible and often made them, and how he was always hanging over the dugout rail when the game was on the line, the way the camera kept showing him clapping, cheering on his teammates.

When Alter came up in the fifth, he hit into a double play. Ouch. Maybe the pressure was getting to him.

✳ ✳ ✳

Pop came home before Dad. They used to both stay out really late the first night, but Pop had gotten to be kind of set in his ways when it came to his bedtime.

I asked, "So, what do you think? How do they look?"

"You tell me. What did you and Zeke see in your before videos?"

"We filmed ten," I said. "But it's only the first day, right? They're not supposed to look good."

"That bad, huh?" Pop asked. "Here. Chet sent these back for you." He offered me a plate of brownies. I took two. "Did you see any promise?" he asked.

"One guy was pretty decent, seemed to know what he was doing, sort of. His mechanics were off, but I think with training, he'll do okay. He was in Group B."

Pop stretched and pulled off his grungy green cap. He looked older without it. You could pretend there was hair up there when his hat was on, I guess. He stood and rubbed his hip a little. The hip replacement surgery he'd had two years ago acted up a lot, gave him some pain. He'd had a lot of parts replaced. I sometimes wondered what percentage of his body was Original Pop.

"You going to bed, Pop?"

"At the end of the day, you can choose to think about what's tearing you apart or what's holding you together," Pop said.

I knew my punch line. "And you've got lots of screws and spare parts holding you together."

Pop smiled, more with his eyes than his mouth. "I'm calling it a night," he said. "If I can still get up those stairs. You?"

"Alter should get one more at bat. I want to see if he gets a hit — he's hitless so far tonight."

"What's he up to?"

"Twenty-four," I said. I heard Dad come in as Pop nodded, impressed, and then went upstairs.

Dad came into the room, and without even a hello or anything, he just asked, "Did you talk to your mother?"

I shook my head.

He sighed and said, "This is ridiculous, Casey. Your mother is not a villain. You know this situation is not all her fault. And you need to call her."

I had nothing to say.

He looked over at the clock—it was almost eleven—and said, "Tomorrow, then," as he started up the stairs. It was pretty obvious he was disgusted with me.

Not her fault? Yeah, I knew married people got divorced all the time. But I bet that every kid whose parents got divorced felt the way I did. Especially if it was clearly one parent's fault, I bet they all felt like that parent pretty much murdered what had once been known as their family. Just killed it.

I knew she couldn't stand living here, but it's not like Behind the Plate didn't exist before they got married. She knew what she was getting into. It was what she signed up for, wasn't it? Everything—the school, the husband, the kid.

But no. I was not going to think about that.

Nope.

I started to write up the game while I waited for Alter's next at bat. Turkleton, who batted ahead of him, got walked and then stole second. So when Alter finally came up, he was intentionally walked. Streak over. He didn't seem mad when he got to first—he gave a sort of "What are you going to do?" smile right at the camera.

On Deck

IF she had known anything at all, Mrs. Bob the Baker wouldn't have worried so much about talking to me on the first day of middle school. Because there wasn't anything special about it. The second day of middle school had been the exact same thing. And the third. It was really kind of amazing how fast something new could become so boring.

It wasn't that I hated school, but I sure didn't love it. I think I enjoyed going when I was in nursery school, and maybe even the early grades, but somewhere along the line, school became one of those necessary unpleasant things, like shots and dentist visits and shopping. It wasn't worth getting upset over—you'd have to do them anyway. That was something I'd learned from Pop: There's no sense in getting upset about things you can't change.

The best times of the school day were lunch; phys. ed., where they mainly had us running in circles around the school for some reason; and of course, going home. To be honest, my English teacher, Mr. Donovan, wasn't bad either. He sometimes ended a class by reading to us from the newspaper or a cool article he'd found in some magazine or online. At least I was able to keep my eyes open. And it was the only class I had with my friend Charley Haddon.

I was actually paying attention when Mr. Donovan announced that he was the supervisor for the school paper and that the first meeting was tomorrow.

I poked Charley and gave him a look like, *So, you in?* Charley looked back at me like I was asking if he wanted to consider joining the Talk About Embarrassing Hygiene Problems Club.

I was hoping I could trick Zeke into going with me — maybe he could write a column about reality TV shows — but when he got on the bus, he was sort of bursting with needing to tell me about his latest great idea.

"Is Ibbit running BTP the same way he always does?"

"I guess," I said.

"So You Suck, Ump! Day — he'll still have You Suck, Ump! Day?"

"I guess."

"I want to film it," he said, and then waited.

I knew some big response was expected, but all I said was, "Why?"

"Think about it from like a director's point of view, or a TV watcher's point of view—it's a sort of amazing concept."

"I'm not seeing it," I said. I looked out the window to track the bus's progress, but we were only passing by 4-C, Clay Coves Community College; we still had quite a way to go.

"Really? You are so lucky to have me for a friend, to explain stuff like this to you."

The logic of that—the lack of logic of that—would have made me want to scream if I weren't so tired. The bus was always hot, and all I wanted to do was close my eyes for a few minutes. I had to help out at BTP when I got home, and I had at least an hour and a half of homework, and for a second, I thought about what it might be like to have a different best friend. Maybe someone bookish—maybe just for today.

"There'd be no need to explain it to me if you weren't here, because you're the one—never mind. What? Go ahead and explain."

He was on his knees on the seat, like the excitement

of this made him bigger or something. "So picture two students out on the field, calling a game. That's what I'd film first, close-ups of the guy behind the plate and the umpire covering first, right?"

"Okay."

"There's no sound at first, just silence."

"But it's on You Suck, Ump! Day, right?"

"Exactly. Slowly, I'll bring the sound in, beginning it at a really low level, and then louder and louder. Until you realize that there are hundreds of people screaming at these guys. It's like a horror movie or something. But it's better, because it's real."

A seventh-grader sitting in front of us turned around and said to Zeke, "You talk too loud, man." He put his hand of top of Zeke's head and shoved him back so that he was sitting.

Zeke's eyes bugged, and he went to knock the hand away, but the kid had already turned around.

"So that's your big plan? You want to film You Suck, Ump! Day?"

He nodded, really excited.

Then I asked, "And do what with it?" But then I realized—oh, my GOD, You Suck, Ump! Day.

"Zeke," I said, and my no-longer-bus-tired voice must have sounded full of something, because he actually stopped talking. He gave me his nonverbal "Go on," which was kind of a tilt of his head with his eyes wide open.

"No Steamboat."

He gave me an instant replay of his nonverbal "Go on" look.

"There's no one to be in charge of You Suck, Ump! Day. Steamboat's not here."

✳✳✳

You Suck, Ump! Day was one of the things that made Pop and Dad's school unique. Not that I'd been to the other two umpire schools, but I just couldn't imagine anyone but a Snowden thinking of it—inviting everyone in town to come scream at our students when they were trying to make calls on the field. That was the point. That baseball wasn't a quiet game. Students had to learn to stay calm and do their job well even when it was loud and unruly.

And You Suck, Ump! Day was both. Loud. And unruly. One year Franco Spinelli's cousin came from New York. He brought a bag full of rotten tomatoes and started throwing them at students while they were calling plays. It had been so surprising, seeing those red blobs fly through the air and then splat right on a student's shoe. Of course, someone made the mistake of also hitting a senior instructor, Lorenzo Watkins. Lorenzo was not amused.

There was now a no-produce-allowed rule at You Suck, Ump! Day.

It was still a few weeks away, and Dad's students had a whole lot to learn before they were out on the field, trying to figure out how to call a game while a whole town was screaming horrible names at them. But now maybe it wouldn't even happen at all, because for the past few years at least, making sure You Suck, Ump! Day had run smoothly had been Steamboat's responsibility.

Unless. Wait! This could be my big chance, like a step up. Instead of all the little things I did to help keep Behind the Plate running, I could be in charge of something big. Something that really mattered.

As long as Dad would let me.

Sticking the Call

WHEN we got off the bus, Zeke went straight out to the fields to work on the before videos. I went in the house to drop off my backpack. The phone was ringing.

I loved caller ID so much I should have written a poem about it. I had avoided every call from Mrs. Bob the Baker.

Just because my mother decided it was time she played a bigger role in my life, or whatever . . . did that mean I had to think it was a good idea? Because I had been doing just fine without her. Ever since she left and went on her big adventure with her baker boyfriend, I hadn't needed her at all. She could spend all her days and nights with Bob the Baker, and I could spend mine without her.

Really.

It had hurt when it was happening. A way-down-deep hurt—like if you were held underwater far longer than you could stand and then were maybe let up for a second but didn't have time to draw another breath before you were pushed down again. Something like that.

One day in second grade, I had gotten off the bus and my mother wasn't there waiting for me. I wondered if maybe she had some kind of surprise for me inside—why else wouldn't she be there? She had always been there.

When I ran into the house, I saw her sitting at the kitchen table with Bob, the baker who used to deliver rolls and bagels and breads to BTP each morning. My mother jumped up and started clearing their plates. She practically yelled, "Why are you home so soon? Why are you home so soon?" It had freaked me out that she'd said it twice.

Bob the Baker left quickly through the back door.

I would never forget the way she concentrated so hard on cleaning all the crumbs off the table, not looking at me the whole time. She put a snack on the table, right in front of me, and left the room.

Not long after that, she told my father she was in love with Bob the Baker. And that she couldn't stand living at Behind the Plate another minute, with all its rules and people in and out of our lives and noise on the fields all day and a husband who was not really available to her during the five weeks of Academy and every last thing about it. She didn't even want to keep the books anymore, which is what they called it when she handled the money. She left us to go live with that stupid baker, and I stayed with Dad. And Mrs. G. had another job added to her long list — bookkeeping.

Most kids I knew with divorced parents lived with their mothers. But I guess it must have seemed obvious to everyone that I belonged at BTP. When the lawyers worked out everything about the divorce, they said I was supposed to spend time with her too, but I just couldn't.

In the beginning, it didn't even matter, because once the divorce was finalized, Mr. and Mrs. Bob the Baker went on some long vacation, sending postcards I refused to read from Florida and Georgia and South Carolina. And then when they came back and tried to make me stay with her on the weekends, I fought and screamed with my dad and refused to talk to my mother or that baker the whole time I was at their stupid house. At some point, they must have gotten tired of fighting with me or maybe she just wanted to see me as much as I wanted to see her — as in not at all.

When I thought about it, I felt that hurt snaking

through me all over again. Which, of course, was why I didn't think about it anymore. Or talk to her either.

You couldn't choose to leave.

Correction: You could choose to leave. But then you couldn't decide you wanted another chance.

Any umpire knew that once you made the call, you had to stick with it.

Stepping Up to the Plate

WHEN I stepped outside to see how Zeke was doing with the videos, I could sense that the place didn't feel as full as it should. It was hard not to think about the guys who were missing — Steamboat, Phillip, To-Go. And twenty or more students. I was worried about this, how there weren't enough students, and what if it was worse next year? What if there were fewer and fewer students? Would the school survive?

You couldn't blame my dad or Pop. You had to blame New Jersey.

Poor New Jersey. It got blamed for so much already. But the other umpire schools were in Florida, where you could hold class in January. In New Jersey, all you could do during January was complain about how long it was until April. New Jersey was the last place you'd want to be if you were interested in doing anything having to do with baseball in the winter. Summer was baseball time in New Jersey, but Dad couldn't hold Umpire Academy then either, because our instructors all worked as minor league umpires until around Labor Day. So BTP had to hold its classes in the fall. By the time Dad's top grads got to Cocoa, five months later, I guess they must've forgotten what they'd learned in the fall. The umpires coming out of the Florida schools had just finished their classes; everything was still fresh in their minds. And there you have it: third-best umpire school.

✳✳✳

On my way out to the fields, I stopped by the dining hall. The tables were all empty, but I heard noise from the kitchen. I pushed through the door and saw Chet at the counter, behind a huge tower of meatballs. "Casey!" he said, sort of pointing at me with his chin, to let me know a high-five with a meatball-handed chef was out of the question. Chet never changed—a big bald guy with kind eyes and a bandanna over his head.

"Those brownies last night were killer."

Chet smiled. I'd almost forgotten how much he liked compliments about his food. Well, duh. Who doesn't like to be complimented about what they do?

"I have some stashed away for your lunch tomorrow," he said.

"Awesome!"

"You wanna help?" he asked.

When I was little, I did sometimes help on meatball night. I liked trying to make them all the same size, perfect spheres of meat. But I was kind of itching to get back to some BTP stuff. "Another time, okay?"

"You got it, chief."

✳✳✳

Students were just finishing up afternoon break, and I could see that they were starting to hang out in groups now. Even June Sponato had found herself a little posse.

Like always, Pop had a group of students gathered around him. Pop had seen a lot in his career as a major league umpire and at all the umpiring jobs he'd had on his way to the big leagues. He said he also learned a lot about umping from teaching it, whatever that means. Anyway, there was often a whole circle around him, nodding. This time one guy was taking notes.

Meanwhile, Dad was talking seriously with someone, in his teacher way, rolling back on his heels as he stood there. I looked closer and realized it was the same guy I'd seen him talking to the past few days.

"Who's that?" Zeke asked.

"I haven't figured out most of their names yet."

Dad looked up, saw me, and smiled. "Hey, Case! Zeke!"

We went over.

"This is Patrick MacSophal. He's already showing a lot of promise."

The guy, a little older and a lot taller than the average student, smiled.

"MacSophal? Like Jimmy MacSophal?" Zeke said.

"Same last name, yeah," the guy said.

"Any relation?" Zeke asked. This guy was clean-shaven and J-Mac had been known for his overgrown beard, so it was hard to tell if there was any family resemblance. When you thought J-Mac, you thought BEARD.

The guy gave a sort of shrug/head-shake gesture and shuffled off.

"Oooooooooooooooookay," Zeke said.

"Well, would YOU want to be related to a pitcher who's only remembered for some steroid scandal?" I said.

"Let it be," Dad said. "We're getting back to work now. Zeke, you finished all the befores?"

"Yup."

"Great. Why don't you go find something to eat, then you can come watch or help or whatever you want."

"How're they looking?" I asked.

"There are some," he said.

"I have to stay at school late tomorrow," I told him while I still remembered.

"You in trouble?

Zeke nodded his head far back and forward.

Pop walked by and swatted him on the head. With all that hair for cushioning, I wondered if he even felt it.

"Just a newspaper meeting," I said.

"Oh, good," Dad said. "You've been waiting for that."

"And also—Steamboat's not here this year," I started.

"I know, Casey. I understand that you're disappointed—"

"Well, no. I mean, I figured you might have forgotten that he's the one who handles You Suck, Ump! Day, and—"

Here Dad slapped his forehead and looked a little nauseated.

"But listen," I continued. "I've got this. I'm going to do it. It'll be the thing I do from now on, okay?"

Dad didn't really have time to say no, or try to think of someone else who could handle it, because students were waiting to do warm-up exercises. Some guys were digging in their bags for sweatshirts. Clouds had rolled in, and the almost-cold in the air reminded me that fall was going to start for real soon.

Dad nodded slowly, like he was still thinking about it while also agreeing to it. "You've got it," he said. "Mrs. G. is usually involved too — talk to her about flyers and anything else you might want. And ask for help if you need it."

Look at us: Zeke was the official A/V guy, and I was running You Suck, Ump! Day. We high-fived, then walked out to the bleachers to watch.

Students were split up onto three different fields. (It was impossible not to think about the fact that in the past we had always needed four fields.)

During the first week of Academy, instructors did a lot of demonstrations. With a mix of students acting as batter, base runners, and fielders, two instructors ran through a bunch of calls in the two umpire positions, as plate ump and base ump. They'd call for the students to act out a certain play, like ground ball up the first-base line with nobody on base. Then everyone watched as instructors showed exactly what position umpires needed to get into. It was something they taught with diagrams in the classroom in the morning, and now, in the afternoon, they put it into play on the field.

After they demonstrated correct positioning and technique a bunch of times, they had students give it a try.

It was always hard to watch at the start of

Academy. A lot of students had a tough time making their feet and arms and head do the right things out on the field, even though they had some experience. Still, it was kind of cool to see them all suited up. They had all the gear on — shin guards, chest protector, mask, cap, strike and ball indicator, the little brush in the back pocket for sweeping off home plate. Dad and Pop believed it was important for students to get used to the feel of all the equipment from the start.

Zeke and I watched the students on field one, but seeing all those feet in the wrong spot, and instructors getting impatient, and field umps being unable to get into the right position to make the call was kind of exhausting. We loved this place more than anything, but even for us, all that stumbling and fumbling wasn't even funny — it was too much. We went to the supply locker, grabbed two gloves and a ball, and went out to the rear field to play catch.

Zeke had terrible form, but he usually managed to get the ball to me. And I didn't mind running after it when he threw it four feet over my head; it didn't matter. The thing about playing catch was, it had more to do with rhythm, ball in glove, transfer to other hand, throw, with the sun in your eyes a little. You didn't need to think when you were playing catch. It was just catch, throw. Catch, throw. Catch, throw. I learned this in the days after Mrs. Bob the Baker left, when Dad and I played catch every night.

It's nice, sometimes, not to think.

Striking Out

Y OU always hear people saying how the hardest thing about journalism is that you have to be objective. I was *born* objective. My family specialized in being objective. It was in the blood. Even if a team was great — your favorite team — that had to disappear when you were an umpire, when you called a game. I totally got that.

When writing an article, you had to show readers the facts, just the facts. It was like standing behind the plate. Umpire and reporter both had to be impartial and fair.

At lunch, I gave it one last shot as I watched Zeke unpack his lunch: a large, unopened box of crackers and a chocolate bar. "I'll give you my sandwich if you'll go to the meeting with me after school."

This got the interest of Charley and Andrew. I was

not generally a lunch sharer—the lunches Chet sent me with were the stuff of legend.

Zeke sort of shook his head with a face that said no way, but still asked, "What did Chet give you? Is it ham, salami, and provolone? Because I think I might be able to make it if it is . . ."

I unwrapped my sandwich and had to catch my breath for a second. I knew it was stupid, but Chet always cut my sandwiches straight across, and today it was cut on the diagonal, the way my mother used to do it. It was like my body was confused, thinking maybe my mother made this sandwich, just like she used to, only I knew that wasn't true. Chet had left the bag for me yesterday afternoon. I didn't feel like crying or anything, but it was a weird moment of emotional and lunch confusion.

I looked in between the slices of bread: "Looks like roast beef today," I said.

"Then I definitely don't have time," Zeke said, as though that made sense. He started feeding crackers into his mouth at an alarming rate. "Ouottarink?" he asked.

"WHAT?" Andrew said.

"Dude, don't ask him what," Charley said, annoyed. "He'll talk more. Look at all that cracker spew. Just wait. Zeke. Chew. THEN talk."

Zeke nodded, like this was the first time such a thing had been suggested and it was a pretty good idea.

"He asked if I had a drink," I explained. "If you get a cup, I'll pour you some of my water. I don't want cracker spew backwash, thank you very much."

Zeke nodded, like of course, he could understand why a person wouldn't want that. For such an agreeable guy, it seemed just mean that he wouldn't come to the meeting with me. "Anyway," he said, "I don't want to stay late at school. Isn't today the day they start working on obstruction and interference? You know I love watching people run into each other."

"But isn't it raining?" I asked. It was hard to tell from the cafeteria, which had no windows, but it had been raining all day. That meant a whole day indoors at BTP—a big group in the lecture hall and then smaller groups in the classrooms. "They're not going to do fieldwork in the rain."

Zeke shrugged. "Rain's gotta end sometime."

✳✳✳

Of course I wasn't able to talk Charley or Andrew or anyone into coming to the meeting with me, so I went alone. The room was full and buzzing with the voices of seventh- and eighth-graders who all seemed to know each other. They were sitting on desks, laughing. I looked around for a familiar face, but there wasn't one. Not one. It was like I'd walked into a meeting for a school newspaper in Toronto or Australia instead of Clay Coves, New Jersey.

I pulled out my English homework and started to read a short story that was originally published in 1918. Of course, given my gene pool, I started to drift, thinking that that year was the last time the Red Sox won the World Series before winning again in 2004. But I was also wondering why Mr. Donovan couldn't assign something slightly more current. Maybe even written in the kind of English that was the same English I knew how to speak.

I was struggling through the second page, going back to the first to see if the author was talking about the same characters or different ones, when Mr. Donovan showed up. With Chris Sykes. The kid who hated me.

"Thank you for coming. It's great to see all your faces back," Mr. Donovan said, looking around the room. He spotted me in the back and added, "And some new ones. A new one." Everyone turned to look at me, and I had the strange desire to dive out the window.

I closed my book and bent to put it away.

"I know you're all anxious to get going, but for our new visitor, I'd like to explain how things work around here. Eighth-graders are pretty much in charge. I am the faculty advisor, and all articles must be approved by me. But to a great extent, this is a student-run enterprise. Eighth-grade students put in their time last year, shadowing last year's editors during spring semester. Seventh-graders will of course play a big role, reporting and editing. We love for new students to take part too. In the spring, Casey, you and any other interested sixth-graders will get a chance to work with upperclassmen on copy editing."

I did not have a poker face—you could almost always tell what I was thinking just by looking at me. My hand wasn't raised, but my confusion must have been right there in my expression.

"You have a question, Mr. Snowden?"

"No. I mean not a question, but it just sounded like—I mean, anyone who wants to write can write, right?"

"Everyone can write for the paper," he said, "once they're in seventh grade." Everyone laughed.

"Wait, what? So in sixth grade, nothing? There's no section or kind of article or anything?" I had been waiting for this forever, and now I couldn't do it? "Do you have, like, a sports section? Maybe we could try to put together a sports . . ."

People were starting to give me looks. Like everyone should know that sixth-graders were supposed to be, what, silent or something?

"Can I speak?" Chris Sykes asked. Mr. Donovan smiled at him and gestured with his hand like, *It's all yours.*

"Sixth-graders get involved by helping us sell advertising space. A lot of local stores have already said they'll buy ads in the *Messenger,* but we're always looking for new ones. We have an advertising kit you can use —"

"What does that have to do with journalism?"

"What?" Chris said, annoyed.

"I mean, I came here because I like to write. I don't like selling stuff. I'd have started a lemonade stand or something if I wanted to sell stuff." I was surprising myself, but there was Chris Sykes, of all people, telling me I couldn't do what I'd been waiting to do since forever!

A few kids laughed. Chris looked pissed. "Why don't you, then? Go open your lemonade stand." I was waiting for him to suggest we hire vampires to squeeze the lemons.

Mr. Donovan put up his hand. Then he said, "This newspaper's a business. Businesses need money, funding."

"It's the way it's always been," Chris said. "When I

was a sixth-grader, it's what I did. It's how I earned my spot."

Was I missing something? "Wouldn't it make more sense to let people who are the best reporters do the reporting and the people who are the best salesmen, or those who like being salesmen, sell ads and stuff?"

I felt a shift in the room. Some kids nudged each other, a few pointed with their chins or the tops of their heads in my direction, in a not-so-positive "Get a load of that kid" kind of way. Or maybe a "When is he going to shut up?" way.

It wasn't exactly the start I had imagined for my journalism career.

"I guess it would be fair to say that no sixth-grader has ever had a story in our paper. That doesn't mean it's impossible. Just very unlikely. It takes time to learn how to write a good article. And you're in the right place to learn. Shifting gears now," Mr. Donovan said. "We're going to have to get a really early start with our first edition, because Chris and Tomas and I have decided that we are going to enter this year's Honorbound Newspaper Competition."

Someone yelled out, "What's that?" but my mind was already wondering why I was even here. I could be back at BTP, in the rhythm of a world I knew and loved, instead of sitting here with people who wondered why I didn't want to walk from store to store asking, "Would you like to buy an ad in our school paper?" I would have joined the Girl Scouts if I wanted to do fundraising. At least then there'd have been good cookies.

Mmm. Thin Mints. Samoas.

Mr. Donovan kept going on about our school's outdated equipment and how, if we won this competition, we'd get a whole new state-of-the-art computer setup. He said the schools that had won in the past had entered really big stories, investigative reporting kinds of things, and we might want to think big, beyond the school's walls. The next meeting would be Monday.

My first thought was to skip that meeting — and all the other ones. But really, even though the whole thing kind of sucked so far, I didn't plan to take no for an answer. No other sixth-grader could have ever wanted it as much as I did. I would be the first.

Touch Base

I WAS sitting on the couch by myself, hoping I might magically think of a perfect article to write for the newspaper — something so good they couldn't turn it down. I looked through my most recent baseball-games notebook, but nothing triggered a great idea.

Dad and Pop banged in through the back door. I heard Pop go straight upstairs. Dad came in the living room and sat right next to me.

He looked at me and said, "Casey, you've got to call your mom. It's not right. She's your mother."

I started to stand up, but he said, "Stop. Now. This is a conversation we need to have."

I wanted to leave. I wanted to be left alone to think of what I was going to write my article about. I wanted to never have this conversation. "What difference does it make to her if she talks to me or not?"

"A big difference."

I blew out some air, a nonverbal way of saying, *Yeah, right.*

"You've broken her heart. She misses you. She wants to talk to you."

If you thought about that, about who broke whose heart, you'd have to say he'd gotten it all wrong.

"Casey, this is hard. I have issues with your mother too, believe me. But you've been acting like she committed a crime. She didn't. This happens to families all the time, doesn't it? Some marriages don't last. But you still have to do what's right. I'm dialing the phone now. And you're staying here. And you're talking to her."

There were times when you could no longer run. Dad dialed and then handed me the phone. Mrs. Bob the Baker answered right away, like she was sitting next to the phone, waiting for it to ring.

"Hello?"

"It's Casey," I said.

She was quiet for a second longer than the normal amount of time and then said, "I'm glad you called."

Dad was still right next to me. I said, "I've been busy."

"Well, it's nice to hear your voice," she said. "I've really missed you."

Sorry. I had no response to that.

"I'd like us to get back into some kind of routine where you come and stay with me."

Oh, no, she did not. She did not just say that.

"I know we never got into a routine at first when I was traveling, and then we weren't that good at making it happen the way it was supposed to once I got back. I didn't want to push. But it's gone on too long like this, Casey, and I want us to spend time together."

"I've been really busy," I said again.

"I'm sure," she said. "Middle school must be a big change for you."

"I guess," I said.

"Well, I'm looking forward to talking with you in person. I'll work it out with your father. Do you want to put him on now?"

No. I did not. So instead of giving her what she was asking for, I gave her something else I knew she wanted: information. "So middle school's kind of different, you know," I said.

"I do! I know! I want to hear all about it. Why don't you plan to come over —"

"I can tell you about it now," I said. My father smiled at me and walked away. I rambled about my classes, and when we were done and she asked me to figure out with Dad what days each week would be good for me to stay with her, I said I would, but I knew I wouldn't.

When we hung up, I was surprised that I felt more relieved than mad. I wasn't dumb enough to believe she'd stop calling. But I had a feeling I'd be free for at least the next week — no screening calls, no threatened visits. I had paid my dues — I'd talked to her.

I'd earned my freedom.

Out of Left Field

ON Sunday morning, the one day I got to sleep late, Zeke didn't start with *hello* or *whazzup*; he just burst into my room with, "So did you ask your dad yet?"

I was sleeping! "About what?" I realized, too late, that I shouldn't have answered.

"You Suck, Ump! Day. If I can film. Does this not ring even a quiet little bell?"

"Quiet little bell?"

"Tell me you asked. And that he said it was okay for me to shoot."

"Izzat Zeke?" my father called in a sleepy voice.

"Hi, Ibbit!" Zeke yelled. Then he mouthed at me, "Should I ask him?"

I pictured him marching into my father's room. *I didn't even go in there.* There was something about seeing how little space he took up on that big bed that I didn't like looking at. I shook my head no. And closed my eyes.

Sometimes if you ignored something, it really did go away.

Only not when Zeke was involved. He was all kinds of determined—a not-normal-eleven-year-old-guy way to act determined—to get something, anything, on TV.

He picked up his camera and started shooting video of me. Instead of telling him to cut it out, I smiled. It was better than him running into Dad's room. It was a Zeke fact I had come to accept—sometimes you had to choose which thing would be less bad for him to do.

"So, You Suck, Ump! Day," he said.

"I don't know, Zeke. He's not going to like it if it seems like you're making fun of his students, you know? And turn that off, okay?"

He put the camera down. "Picture it, okay? BTP has all these students—they've already given photo and video clearance to your dad, right?"

"You know they have, yeah."

"But it wouldn't even matter, because what if I filmed someone from behind? Like no identifying features of any kind. You don't need any special permission to use someone's likeness if they can't tell it's them."

"I just don't think he's going to want negative publicity—"

"There's no such thing as negative publicity. Any publicity I can get for your dad's school is going to be a good thing." Find me another eleven-year-old who says, "There's no such thing as negative publicity." Only someone who watched people make fools of themselves on TV on a regular basis could use language like that.

"Dude. You're sitting there with a straight face, telling me that getting a clip of a BTP student onto *So You Think You're the Biggest Idiot?* is going to do wonders for the image of the least successful umpire school in the country? Come on."

I silenced him. Go, me.

I had to remember, next Saturday night, to lock all the doors so Zeke couldn't do this again.

Still in the Game

YOU'RE back?" Chris Sykes said when I walked into the room after school on Monday. In the same tone of voice he might have used if he had noticed a moth flying out of my ear.

"Good to see you," I said in a weird and confident-sounding voice. Just selling it with a no-doubt-about-it tone, the key to being a good umpire. I'd never pulled that tool out before. But I'd never been told the odds were stacked against me before either.

Mr. Donovan started the meeting. "Pretty soon we're going to need to know how many ads we'll have so we know how many pages we can afford to print. How's everyone doing with ad sales?"

The whole room turned to look at me. Was I *every-one?* I guess not, because a girl in the front row by the window said, "I got Luigi's Pizza to take a quarter page, and my dad said his store will take a full page."

"That's fantastic," Chris Sykes said.

"Nice work," Mr. Donovan said.

"How'd you do, Snowden?" Sykes said.

"I forgot to take that folder of ad-sales information," I said, an answer that wasn't really an answer. An answer that sort of said, *I haven't sold a single ad, and I don't intend to. I want to write for the newspaper, not be an ad salesman.*

"You know what? Your attitude's crap. Why don't you just get out?" Chris said.

"I don't think so," I said.

Shouldn't Mr. Donovan defend me? I wasn't doing anything wrong. I just wanted to write news stories. And this *was* a school newspaper meeting.

Mr. Donovan put up his hands in a let's-have-peace-here kind of way. "The folders are on that desk, Casey," he said. "Chris, why don't we move on."

I went to the back of the room and found a folder, and tried to stay there until the conversation resumed. But there was this big pile of silence just sitting in the room.

So I turned around, walked back to the desk, and said, "I still have a question. If I wrote an article that was better than anything anyone else wrote, maybe something that you thought could win that Honorbound Competition, would it even get considered? Or do you really believe that sixth-graders can't write as good as eighth-graders?"

"As well," Mr. Donovan said.

I sighed.

"Wow, seriously?" Chris Sykes said, all huffy. "You think you're so great. Like you're going to come in here and be better than kids two years older than you? Get over yourself, Snowden."

"Let's move on to preliminary assignments now," Mr. Donovan said.

"Excuse me," I said. Or at least, I thought it was me. I had always been good with following rules. Maybe you picked up on this already, but I grew up at an umpire school. I believed in rules. And here I was, the kid in the classroom who wouldn't shut up, who kept challenging the rules. "What about my question? Would you really turn away a great article only because someone in sixth grade wrote it?"

Mr. Donovan looked like he'd rather be, well, anywhere, I guess. Not here. Not dealing with me.

"I can't speak hypothetically. Until I see an article, I just . . . I don't have any answers for you."

That was not an option in baseball. Imagine it: The pitcher throws some heat. Did it catch the outside corner? It was close. The pitcher's looking in, waiting for the call. The batter turns around. The ump flips up his mask and shrugs, saying, "I don't have any answers for you."

Middle school was not like umpire school.

Players Take the Field

ON the late bus home, I read through the Honor-bound Competition notes and examples of papers and articles that had won in the past few years. They weren't what I thought they would be. They seemed like they could be in a regular paper, not some school newspaper. They weren't about the lousy food in the cafeteria or the amazing come-from-behind win staged by the boys' track team.

One of the articles was about how all the schools in that district were in violation of the town's fire code. How did a student figure that out? And one was an undercover story, or something like that, where this kid figured out that a company in his town was dumping illegal stuff in a big lake. And one had an interview, a really good one, with an ex-senator, where the senator didn't only talk about all the important things he had done, but also the things he wasn't able to do, and the mistakes he made. That was my favorite article. You didn't usually see important people like that admitting they'd ever done anything wrong. It was sort of doubly cool that it was in a student newspaper.

I told Zeke all about it when I got to BTP. They were doing outside drills, and Zeke was sitting on the low wall that ran behind the batting cages. "I just need a good idea," I told him, kind of hoping he'd hand me one.

But instead of lingering around like he always did, he said, "Good luck with that. I've gotta go," and jumped on his skateboard. "History project's due tomorrow."

Dad saw me and motioned that it was okay to come in and sit with him and the staff behind the judging table.

Instructors were calling out situations that could occur in a game (like man on second, two outs), and other instructors and some students were putting those plays into action on the field. Working in teams of two — one ump behind the plate and the other in the field, plate ump and base ump — students tried to make the right calls on the plays. (Because only the major leagues used four umpires, all schools taught the two-umpire system.)

Just like in a game, students had no idea where or if the ball would be put in play, so they had to be ready to make any call. To watch, read the play the right way, remember which umpire needed to make each call, get into the correct position, and make the right call with all the right body movements, or mechanics.

Billy and Joe, two guys Dad had hired when they were baseball players at Clay Coves Community College and who had come back every September since, were working with Dad and Bobbybo and Soupcan and half the students. Pop had the other half on the rear field, along with some other instructors.

I watched Dad's group. It wasn't pretty. There was a man on first, and instead of covering third on a hard hit to the outfield, the plate ump took off his mask and just kind of stood there, watching the ball. The base ump wasn't much better. He was able to run to the right position to call the play, but he didn't get there in time to position himself at the best angle. And when he got the angle right, he was too far away to make a good call on the throw to first.

Dad and the other instructors watched each student run through about ten different situations, and then the students were called over to the outfield to listen to what they had done right and what they had done wrong. It was one of the things I liked least about

BTP — the way students had to stand there and be told that that their feet weren't set far enough apart or they blew a catcher's interference call. I didn't think I could handle that part if I were a student here. I understood they needed feedback to know what they had to work on, but who really wanted to hear about all the things they were lousy at? You had to look the instructors in the eye and nod, like, *Yeah, I want to hear this! What else did I do wrong? Okay, what else? Thank you, sir, may I please have another?*

When Dad came back to the table after a face-to-face evaluation, I asked, "Do you know how I can reach Steamboat? I want to talk to him about You Suck, Ump! Day, find out everything I need to do."

"Check with Mrs. G.," he said. Which I probably could have figured out for myself.

I reached back behind where Dad was sitting and opened the cooler. He was so predictable. There were three bottles of iced tea and tons of packs of sunflower seeds. I grabbed one of each and headed to the rear field, where Pop was sitting in the bleachers behind home plate.

I climbed up next to him.

He pushed his green hat back and scratched his forehead while pointing with his chin to the plate ump. "What do you think of that one, Casey?"

I watched for a minute. He was kind of clumsy pulling his mask off. That was one of the first lessons they got about their uniforms — how to hold the mask, how to put it on, take it off. They were supposed to always have their heads up, staring out at the field (almost staring down the players) as they put on their masks. No matter what he was doing, an umpire's eyes always had to be up and facing forward.

Pop held a ball and strike indicator as he watched this guy, and he was turning its dials without a break. I had forgotten about that — that was what Pop did when a student was making him crazy.

This guy's crouching position seemed right. His feet were spread wide, he had one hand below his chest protector and the other above his knee, his chin was above the catcher's head, and he was holding his head steady. He was the right distance from the catcher. He was a little slow, though, standing up to make the call once the pitch was made, almost like he had to think about it. It had to be automatic. Pop and Dad were really strict about position and mechanics. This student's voice was a little quiet too.

"A little tentative," I said.

"A little?" Pop said with a smile.

Umpires need to be convincing. To speak with authority. Everyone on the field — and even in the stands — need to feel like umpires are in charge, like the game is under control. I felt like I was born knowing that, because it was the main thing they preached here, from the first day until the last.

"I've been telling this kid to sell the call. We worked on that yesterday, but this one doesn't seem to have it in him." Pop put down the ball and strike indicator and scribbled something on the guy's evaluation sheet in one of the big binders.

"Pendrikston! Make the next call as loud as you can, the loudest you can call it." He picked up the indicator again.

The student looked up at Pop and nodded his head really fast. He turned back and got into position. Once the ball hit the mitt, he called, "Strike!" It was pretty loud.

"Now make the next one louder than that," Pop said, spinning the dials on the indicator like crazy.

I thought about all the homework I had to do. I was getting up when Pop surprised me with a question. "What do you think you're going to do, years from now, when you're all finished with school?"

The seriousness in his face when he was talking to Pendrikston completely, instantly melted away when he talked to me.

"You know that, Pop," I told him. "Be a reporter."

"What about this place? Do you think you'll want to keep on at this place?"

"Of course. That's like asking if I think my blood will always be part of my body."

Pop smiled, then turned to the field and yelled, "Okay, Pendrikston. You and Turner switch out. Turner, behind the plate!"

"I'll always be here, Pop. And I'll be a reporter too. I don't know how to make that happen, but I'm twelve, right? Not supposed to have all the answers yet, I hope."

"The future may not give you everything you want," Pop said, watching as the two students got into position on the field. "But Snowdens are determined. I bet your future gives you everything you need and most of what you want. That's what I hope for you."

"Thanks, Pop. I better do some homework, or I won't have a future."

Pop laughed and then started yelling at Turner, "What kind of position is that? Look at your feet! Is that how your feet are supposed to be?"

I went inside and found a pad and paper. I needed a solid story idea. It had to be better than good—the very best I could do. I wished articles were submitted without names on them, because there was no way anyone was going to judge anything I wrote fairly anyway.

I sat under a tree near the parking lot and turned to a blank sheet and wrote the words *Story Ideas.*

Then I stared into space for fourteen hours. At least it felt like it. This was one of those times when I wished Dad weren't so busy, so he could sit down with me and think. But the five weeks of Academy were always like this. Just as I was ready to start feeling a little sorry for myself, Soupcan came and stood in front of me. "Hey, Case," he said. "What're you up to?'

"Trying to come up with ideas for the school newspaper, but I can't think of anything."

"Could you write something about this place?"

Soupcan used to be famous for sneaking off to take cigarette breaks, but for the past few years, he'd been famous for trying to quit smoking. He said that coming to BTP always seemed like the perfect chance to try to leave a nasty habit behind. The fact that *always* was in that sentence showed that he had not been terribly successful. I checked his hand. He was clean. Some guys from his group were lined up at the cooler for drinks. "It's not really news," I said. "You know? It's a *news*paper."

He nodded.

"Actually, it's like the stupidest thing, because I'm in sixth grade and they have never even published an article by a sixth-grader, so I'm not even sure why I'm bothering."

"Because it's what you want to do." He pulled a toothpick out of his back pocket, put it in his mouth, and started chewing on it. "It's what you've always wanted to do, as long as I've known you."

"I'm trying to come up with an idea so great they have to publish it."

"Something they can't refuse," he said, spitting the toothpick onto the grass and reaching into his back pocket for a piece of gum. "Want one?"

"No, thanks."

"You know, You Suck, Ump! Day is coming up. Maybe you could write about that."

"Everyone in Clay Coves already knows about it."

Soupcan was quiet for a minute, chewing. "I have two thoughts on that," he finally said. "First, it's like umpiring in some ways, isn't it? The way it's always the same game, on paper. But some guys just know how to call a game. There's a difference between a game called by a pro and one called by a hack — an obvious difference. So maybe it's not the game, it's how you call it. Maybe writing's like that."

I thought about that, then asked, "And what's your second thought?"

"There was a second thought? Man, I need a smoke." He took the wrapper his gum had been in, spit the gum out, and put it back in his pocket. Gross. "The second thing, come to think of it, is kind of the same as the first. It's not what you write about. It's how you write it. I love baseball, but there are some baseball writers I can't stand. I'd rather read about, I don't know, sewer construction, than read what they have to say about baseball." He stuck a new toothpick into his mouth. "And there are some writers whose articles I read no matter what, even if the subject doesn't interest me. Because they're such good writers."

This was, by far, longer than any conversation I'd ever had with Soupcan. I liked what he was saying. "Thanks," I said. I *was* a good writer. Whenever I read through my stories about World Series games—I'd written up every postseason game for the past three years—I couldn't imagine anyone reading them and not loving them. Not that it was hard to write well about something as exciting as a championship game.

"You coming back?" Hank Lorsan yelled over. Soupcan waved and turned to me. "Did that help?"

I nodded.

"Excellent," he said, looking a little surprised. "Good luck."

a Whole New Ball Game

WHEN Zeke got on the bus, it seemed like he was almost bouncing down the aisle to me. I sent a silent bit of thanks out into the universe that Zeke was not someone entrusted with extremely important secrets like, say, having to do with national security, because we'd all be in trouble. He held a story he wanted to tell almost the same way a puppy holds joy — with lots of wiggling and moving parts.

He sat next to me. In fact, he sort of sat on top of me, but then he shifted over. "You won't believe this. You won't."

"Okay," I said.

"There's no such person as Patrick MacSophal."

"Oh. Okay. So that person named Patrick Mac-Sophal, the one I saw running laps around the rear field before I came to school this morning, he's actually —"

"J-Mac!"

"Right," I said. "A former major league pitcher is attending the least good umpire school in the country. And he's using a fake first name. And why is he doing that?"

"To sell drugs to the umpire students?"

"What are you *talking* about?" I must have started speaking loudly because the seventh-grader who always sat in front of us turned around. I think he knew it was me, but he swatted Zeke on the head anyway.

"I haven't figured out the why yet. But I went online, and J-Mac doesn't have any brothers. He's an only child."

"That's your big proof?" I said. "Don't become a lawyer. I am almost certain that you need to have more than one unrelated fact to prove a case. This is just . . . so what, Zeke?"

"Listen," Zeke said. "This guy shows up. Admits he's a relative of J-Mac's, right?"

"Well, doesn't deny it," I said.

"He looks just like him, right?"

"Does he? I mean, I know a person can shave a beard, but who even paid attention to what he looked like behind all that face hair?"

"Case, it's not like there's a twin walking around.

No siblings. Only child. Born and raised in Portland, Oregon."

"So maybe it's a cousin or something," I said.

Then, for no good reason at all, I started thinking, what if it really was him?

The whole J-Mac scandal had really, really bugged me. I didn't like the way baseball got a bad name because of all the rumors about players using drugs. Steroids, all that stuff. It started when that big superstar, Reggie Rhodes, got busted. His blood test showed he'd been using steroids. It was big news. When they asked where he'd gotten the drugs, Rhodes claimed he didn't know he'd taken drugs, he had just helped himself to what he thought was herbal stuff from J-Mac's locker. There was going to be this whole big investigation, but instead of clearing his name or explaining what had happened, J-Mac, this youngish star-on-the-rise relief pitcher, had vanished.

"I wanna find out what happened to J-Mac, don't you? I mean, people don't just disappear."

"Zeke. It wasn't magic. J-Mac didn't disappear for real. He just left baseball. Maybe he got a job at a bank. Or he's working as a janitor somewhere."

"Don't you think it's weird, though? Not trying to defend yourself?"

I shrugged. I didn't really know what to think. Some relative, some connection to that old mystery, might be at BTP. I had to admit it was kind of interesting.

But in the end, it didn't really matter. There were no second chances in baseball. You could read *The Snowden Guide to Umpiring* a hundred times, and you'd never come to a section titled "Do-Overs."

Not Quite on the Ball

COULDN'T explain why I did it. The next morning, from the privacy of my own room, where I couldn't be seen, I watched MacSophal jogging around the rear field. I opened the window and yelled out, "Hey, J-Mac," and he looked up right away.

Now, I don't know about you, but I don't answer to other people's names.

***

Waiting for the bus to get to Zeke's stop, my foot was tapping and my fingers were sort of scratching the seat; I was anxious to tell him what I'd learned.

And I did, the minute he sat down. "So when I yelled it, no hesitation or anything, he just looked right up."

"Well, I'd normally think that was proof, except it was early morning, and it's weird to hear a voice yell, right? Maybe he was trying to figure out who was making the noise."

How had we gotten here? When, exactly, did the world turn upside down? I was acting like Zeke. And he was shooting holes in my theory—acting like me.

"You know what this means, right?" Zeke said.

"That I shouldn't hang out with you so much." The bus pulled into the long driveway. Another day of school.

"We have a mystery to solve. Let's think about it this morning and discuss our strategy at lunch, okay?"

"Um, no." There was no way an MLB star pitcher was ever going to be taking classes at BTP. It made no sense. I walked off the bus, feeling like a moron for screaming a major league ballplayer's name out my bedroom window. I had a mostly functioning brain. How had I let Zeke convince me of this? This was like pretending our very own mailman was Joey Collins of *That'sPETacular* all over again.

The morning dragged on, as mornings do in school. But then, lunch! Some days it was almost as good as vacation. Sometimes it was just what I needed, to sit down with my friends and let my brain stop thinking for a while.

I found Zeke at our table with Charley Haddon and Evan Bergino and sat across from him. I opened my Chet-packed lunch. A bagel with cream cheese, two big chocolate chip cookies, water, and some cut-up watermelon. It sure beat middle-school cafeteria food.

I waited for the fun of Zeke unveiling his lunch. Yesterday he'd had three peanut butter granola bars, and one day last week, he brought in two eggs that were hard-boiled and one that wasn't. That was literally the funniest mess I had ever seen.

He opened his bag and pulled out two apples and a drink.

"That looks like lunch for a pony," I said.

"Good one," he said. "But until you get Chet to start making my lunch, you don't get to comment. This is what we had this morning. Anyway, did you come up with any ideas for proving that it's really J-Mac?"

I unwrapped the bagel and started eating. "No. Listen. I don't want to ruin your fun or anything, but I think I just got caught up in . . ." There was no nice way to say *your insanity,* so I just looked at him. But he was still waiting for more info. "I mean, it's not J-Mac. And even if it is, so what, right? It's like getting excited because there's a criminal in your neighborhood. The guy's just a cheater, not some Cy Young Award winner."

"So you *do* think it's him!"

"I don't think it's him. That's the main point. But

the subpoint, if you will, is that even if it is J-Mac, I don't want to know."

"I do." He put down the core of one apple and bit into the second. "Do you remember that joke about what's worse than biting into an apple and seeing a worm, and the answer's seeing half a worm?"

"Yeah," I said.

"That's a good one," he said.

Wow.

"So anyway, I have a plan. Today after school, when everyone's doing outdoor drills, I'm going to sneak into the dorm, find his ID, and prove it."

"First of all, no. You're not. My dad would kill you and then he would kill me for being the reason he knows you and had to kill you."

The lucky thing about being Zeke's friend for so long is I know he says he's going to do a ton of things that he never really does. Which is good. Because his ideas can be terrifying.

"Second of all?" he said after a weird pause.

"And second of all, just no."

"Yeah, I'm totally sneaking into his dorm room," Zeke said. "And you're coming with me."

Illegal Play

I WISH I had like a cat-burglar suit," Zeke said as we walked toward the dorms. We hadn't even said hi to my dad yet. Zeke believed—and he was probably right—that my dad had no idea what time I got home from school and wouldn't notice if we got out to the fields ten minutes later than usual. But this, sneaking into a student's room, was really something Zeke shouldn't do. Why didn't he know that?

"MacSophal's in Group H, right?" he said.

"I'm not answering. The whole reason I'm here is to get you to stop doing what you're doing. And you know what? Why don't we just go play catch or something? I'll even let you pitch. From the mound."

I never offered that, because it meant chasing a ball all afternoon, but I was feeling a little desperate. I had definitely gotten his attention, because he stopped walking. But then he said, "Nah. I just need you to be my lookout."

"No," I said. "Seriously, you could get me into a lot of trouble with this, and I really —"

"Hiiiii!" we heard. And then saw. Sly. Oh, I felt like maybe I loved her in that moment. She was a little one-girl superhero, whose superpower was the ability to rescue me from my best friend's bad judgment.

"Hello, Sylvia," Zeke said. "Where's your grandma?"

"It's Sly," she said.

"Don't you have school today?" I asked. I had stopped following Zeke and was standing right behind the school office's back door — so happy to not be walking toward the dorms. And trouble.

"I did, yeah."

I could see Zeke beginning to tense up, like a supercharged energy ball, desperate to get away.

"But doesn't elementary school end at three fifteen?" I asked, determined to make this conversation last forever.

"I go to St. Luke's now," she said, as though that explained everything. "What are we doing?"

"Important and dangerous things," Zeke said and began to walk away. I didn't follow.

"I'll help," she said.

"Do you want Sly to help?" I asked Zeke in an innocent voice. "That's a pretty good idea. Sly could totally help us."

"No, that's okay," Zeke said. "Come on, Casey, let's let her, uh, do homework."

"No, listen," Sly said. "I have no homework, which is weird, but I'm really happy. So let me help you guys."

"No," Zeke said.

"Well, I'm coming," she said, and started walking toward him.

"Whatever," he said.

And they both took off.

Great.

So now I was following two clowns instead of one and wondering if it was even possible to keep this from turning into a huge disaster. Like it wasn't bad enough getting in trouble with Zeke—now I had to be responsible for turning Mrs. G.'s granddaughter into a criminal.

"I got a cat," Sly said. The kid was random. I usually enjoy random. I like Zeke, don't I?

"If you're coming, you have to be silent," Zeke said.

"No, I don't," Sly said.

"Then don't come."

"I'm coming, and I'm talking, and I got a cat."

"Great," I said, speed-walking to catch up.

Zeke walked into the back door of the dorm. "Which room?" he asked me. I was pretty sure it was on the second floor, somewhere in the middle, but I wasn't about to make this easy for him.

"So when we first got Tiny—that's my cat's name, because he's tiny? So when we first got him, my mom was sneezing a lot, and I was just thinking that it reminded me so much of that *Brady Bunch* episode? The one where Jan keeps sneezing whenever she's near Tiger? Do you know the *Brady Bunch*? My grandma got me all the DVDs. Except on that *Brady Bunch* episode? It's not Tiger she's allergic to? It's Tiger's flea powder? Except they don't realize that until it's almost too late? And the dog's going to have to leave the family? But then they—"

"Sylvia?" Zeke said.

"SLY!"

"If you're coming with us, Sly, you must accept that this is a silent mission."

She made a face.

"But I want to talk to you about your cat later. Would you like to try to get your cat on TV?"

I saw Sly's jaw drop, and at that moment, I saw a

way out, like a lit-up neon arrow pointing away from trouble. "Why don't we talk about that now?" I said.

"You know what? Forget it. I don't need help here. Casey, you and Sly can hang here. I'm going to go up by myself and see if I can figure out which room is his, and—"

"Which room is whose?" Sly asked. "My grandma knows all this stuff. I can help."

Oh, great. So now Sly was starting to understand what we were doing. "Nice work," I said. "Listen. Let's just say Mission Aborted, okay? This is a bad idea. I can feel it, you know?" I tilted my head toward Sly, raising my eyebrows. I realized my shoulders were practically in my ears—I was all scrunched up with nerves and fear. Fear of my best friend.

"What? I don't get what you guys are talking about."

Zeke turned and headed up the stairs, but I called after him, "I have a better way of finding out, but you have to stop what you're doing now." After a few seconds, I heard his feet slowly coming back down.

"What's your plan?" he said.

"Yeah," Sly said.

Excellent question. I had no plan. This was what was known as bluffing. "Not now," I said with a slight tone of mystery in my voice. Zeke nodded knowingly.

Then I asked, "Sly, how old's your cat?"

"I don't know," she said. "He's a baby to me, because we just got him, but the vet says he's three, which isn't really a baby."

Zeke's eyes were about to roll back in his head — he was never known for his patience.

"So Zeke," I asked, "how are you going to get Tiny on TV?"

Getting the Call Right

AFTER Zeke left, with plans made for me to help him shoot video of Sly's cat, I went to talk to Mrs. G. about You Suck, Ump! Day. She was pouring a ton of white powder — fake milk, I think — into a big cup of coffee.

"Dad said you could order the You Suck, Ump! Day flyers for me. Do you know how many and stuff?"

Mrs. G. nodded and looked through a file cabinet. "I'll take care of that. And you might want to look through this," she said, handing me a thin file with a few papers in it.

"Thanks. Do you know how I can reach Steamboat?"

She frowned. Then nodded again. "I have his phone number somewhere." She opened a couple of drawers and then closed them. "It should be . . ." I expected her to reach into her bun and pull something out, but she turned to a bulletin board and found a crumpled piece of paper with lots of names and numbers. "Here it is," she said, copying the number onto a piece of paper for me.

"Thanks."

I went back outside. Students were working on different fields, reviewing angles for viewing plays and taking turns making the "He's off the bag!" call. On field two, Jorge Washington and the guy I thought was Lincoln Cabrera were standing next to each other, watching students race down the line.

A lot of people believe the most important umpiring goes on behind the plate. Of course balls and strikes, and calling them right, is a big deal. But the most important part of being an umpire is being in the right position to make the call. You need to get to where the play is going to be made and pretty much stand at a right angle to that exact spot — close enough to see, but not so close that you get in any player's way.

Pop had a friend, when he was umping in the majors, who missed a call. That happens sometimes, of course. But this guy called a player safe when he was out, and it was the only at bat scored as a hit in the entire game. So that pitcher's only shot in his whole career at throwing a no-hitter was taken away from him all because Pop's friend missed the call. Pop told me that when I was a little kid, and it stayed with me, how important it is to make the right call. How you only get one chance.

Today Pop wasn't even trying to hide how disgusted he was with some of the students' techniques. He kept yelling, "You can't make a long-distance call! Hustle faster!" or "Tell your happy feet to stay still." I could see his hand practically crushing a ball and strike indicator.

I looked over at field four, empty, and wondered what that meant for next year. It was hard for BTP to compete. If you had to choose between spending five weeks in Florida or five weeks in New Jersey — well, do the math.

On field one, students were in all player positions, except Lorenzo was pitching, and Bobbybo was batting. He was hitting shots to different field positions with the fungo bat, seeing if the field and base ump would remember where to go to make the call.

He hit one to right field, and the guy who was playing there caught it and gunned it home. I mean, he really gunned it. A few guys whistled, and Lincoln and Washington started slow-clap applauding and then did some long and complicated high-five, complete with wiggly fingers. The student working as base runner, trying to score from third, was out by a lot, and he looked shocked. We didn't usually see arms like that here.

"That was some throw!" Bobbybo called out. "You've got a major league arm!"

The right fielder tipped his cap. It was Patrick MacSophal.

Out of My League

I SHOULDN'T have been on the stairs in the first place. I hardly ever got hungry in the middle of the night, but I was starving. Like crazy, could-never-fall-asleep-if-I-didn't-eat starving. Almost chew-off-one-of-my-own-limbs starving. So I started heading downstairs. I knew it was really late—the last time I'd looked at my clock it was after midnight.

Dad was talking to someone. I thought it was Pop, since, well, he was the only other person who lived here, but that was weird. I mean, Pop hadn't been up after eleven (except for postseason games on TV) for as long as I could remember. Then again, I wasn't usually up after midnight either.

I moved down a few more steps, but didn't go near

the one right before the landing — that one squeaked no matter where you stepped.

I sat and listened. And I'll never forget what I heard.

It was Dad. Talking. I figured out pretty quickly that the person he was talking to was "Patrick" MacSophal.

"Baseball's been my whole life," MacSophal said. "I love the game. It's all I've ever wanted to do. So when it ended, I didn't know what to do with myself. I had enough money that I didn't really need to decide right away. I went home, spent some time with my folks, my girlfriend. Tried to figure out what my next step should be. In some ways, I think I'm still trying to figure that out."

"A lot of us could say the same thing." Dad said.

"What do you mean?" MacSophal asked. "It seems like you've got everything in order here. A pretty good life."

Yeah, I thought. *What do you mean?*

"Don't get me wrong," Dad said. "I love what I do. I love my life. What I don't love is . . . not being more successful at it."

"I still don't get what you're saying."

"Well, why did you come here, to *this* school, instead of one of the Florida schools?" Dad asked.

"So what you're saying is you wish this place was one of the top-ranked schools?"

"Answer *my* question," Dad said.

He always sounded like a teacher. And like a dad. He wasn't letting this guy get away with anything. If he'd been standing, he'd have been rolling back on his heels.

"I'll answer yours if we can get back to mine."

There was one of Dad's famous teacher pauses and then he surprised me with, "Okay. Fair enough."

"I came here because I thought I had the best chance of flying under the radar."

"I suppose that makes good sense. And to answer yours: Of course I wish my school were more successful—who wouldn't want to be successful?" It was quiet for a minute and then Dad asked, "So when did you start thinking about umpiring?"

"When I couldn't find any other way back into baseball. I couldn't even get a college coaching job back home. My name's mud."

If Zeke had been there, he'd have been unable to resist putting out his hand and saying, "Hi, Mud. Nice to meet you." But that's not exactly right, because what he would really have been doing was jumping up and down on the creaky step, screaming, "I TOLD YOU THIS DUDE WAS J-MAC!!!"

"And no offense to your school intended, but I figured I had a better chance of being recognized if I went to one of the Florida schools."

"Even if you used this new name?"

"I used my given name on the application. My father's a Patrick, too, so everyone always used my middle name, called me Jimmy. The J-Mac thing sort of happened in the papers when I had that great streak. I pitched seventeen scoreless innings, and I guess that's when the papers decided I needed a nickname. But here, I wanted people calling me Patrick, not MacSophal. I want to stay out of the spotlight, you know?"

"There's one thing I don't understand, Patrick: Why didn't you ever try to clear your name?"

"You want the truth?" MacSophal said.

I held on to the step. I did not want to fall. I did not want to make a noise. I did not want to risk this moment not happening. Imagine the headline: KID MAKES STEP SQUEAK, MISSES STEROID-USER'S CONFESSION.

Dad must have nodded or something, because MacSophal kept talking. "I couldn't. I've used. And I have a lot of friends who have too. Steroids, growth hormone, amphetamines. I probably know more players who did than who didn't."

Dad was silent.

"Getting myself into a whole lot of trouble—that I could handle. Maybe. But I could not bring down my friends. So when Rhodes named me, it seemed like the honorable thing to do was just disappear."

My mouth was literally open. I wanted to yell, *Honorable? How can a drug-taking cheater be talking about what's honorable and what isn't?*

"But enough about me. Tell me what you think about having the third-ranked school in the country."

"Out of three," Dad added.

MacSophal laughed a little.

"It's how my life works right now," Dad said.

"Do you dream of more?"

"Sometimes," Dad said.

"Why don't you move the school to Florida, compete head-to-head with the others?"

"My life is here."

"You mean your kid?"

"Among other things."

"But what if you did Academy down there and kept the other classes, the school, your life here the rest of the time?"

"Five weeks is a long time for a kid."

"He's not really a little kid. Isn't there someone who could take care of him for five weeks?"

There was a very long pause while I waited for my dad to explain that Pop would need to come to the school with him too, so really, I'd be all alone at home, and of course he couldn't do that. And then Dad said, "You know? There might be."

He didn't have to say that it was Mrs. Bob the Baker. I knew. I also knew it could never, ever happen.

Little League

I DIDN'T sleep. Or at least I didn't think I did. My brain was all over this MacSophal thing. How could my dad allow that cheater to attend his school? And how could this cheater be telling my dad it was okay to go to Florida for over a month, every year, without me?

I wanted to talk to someone about this, but I couldn't tell Zeke. The potential for him to do something stupid with this information was too great, so I decided to wait and keep thinking. Which I would have liked to do at home. But Zeke had decided this would be the day we filmed Sly's cat.

So there we were in front of Mrs. G.'s house on a Saturday afternoon — me with my bike and Zeke with his skateboard. Sly was waiting for us with a big cardboard box on her lap.

"You're not going to hurt him, are you?"

"Of course not," Zeke said. "Definitely not on purpose, anyway."

Sly stood and started carrying the box back to the house.

"I'm kidding!" Zeke said. He looked at me and said, "Kids!" Then he asked Sly, "So what tricks does your cat know?

"He's supposed to know tricks?"

"Unless it's some kind of stupid cat."

Sly looked stunned. I think Zeke really didn't get that you couldn't talk to little kids the same way you talked to . . . people. Or maybe it was that Sly was a girl? Or some combination. I was definitely not Sly's biggest fan, but he shouldn't have been mean to the kid when she was trying to help him out.

"Hey, boys," Mrs. G. called from the front steps, her hair hanging down instead of in that holding-pencils-and-other-surprises bun. "It's so nice of you to come over to play with Sylvia today."

Sly just mouthed the word "Sly."

"Actually, we're really just —"

I cut Zeke off. "We wanted to meet her cat!" I said. You have to know how to play the old people. You didn't tell them that you wouldn't be caught dead here if it weren't for the fact that your slightly off-in-the-head best friend was trying to get something — anything — on TV and that he'd decided her granddaughter's cat just might be the ticket. And you definitely didn't mention that eleven- and twelve-year-old guys did not play with eight-year-old girls in any universe anywhere, ever.

"It's probably a good thing she's taken the cat out of the house. Her mom starts sneezing whenever she's near him."

Zeke gasped and put his palm flat on his cheek. "That is JUST like Marcia Brady!" he said.

"Jan, you idiot," Sly said.

"Please be careful. It's a busy street," Mrs. G. said before going inside.

The Concerns of the Old, a list by Casey Snowden:
1. It's a busy street.
2. You could take someone's eye out with that thing.
3. Now you're laughing; soon you'll be crying.
4. Turn on a light! How can you read in that dark room?
5. Wash your hands before you eat!
6. Move back from the television! You're way too close!
7. You can't swim; you just ate.

I always wondered at what age you officially got old

and started saying stuff like that—it was somewhere between Dad and Pop. I had to remember to write it down the first time I heard Dad talking like an old person.

"So really, now," Zeke said to Sly. "What does your cat do?"

"He eats. He sleeps. He can arch his back that way that cats do. He poops. And pees."

Zeke gave me a look like, *THIS is what I have to work with?*

"What do the animals do on *That'sPETacular?*" I asked Zeke.

"*That'sPETacular?* I love that show! Oh, my God! Tiny's going to be on *That'sPETacular?* I can't believe it! Oh, my God! Thank you so much!"

Zeke shook his head and sat on his skateboard. "I have no idea if your cat will get on. We might have to teach her some tricks or something. Can we at least see her?"

I wondered if trouble was coming. What if the cat ran away? "Has she been outside before?" I asked. I'd never had a pet, but if I were stuck inside all the time, told to eat out of a bowl on the floor, to do my business in a little box where everyone could see, I'd run away the first chance I got.

"Yeah," Sly said. She opened the box and pulled

out a black and white cat. Tiny blinked a few times, getting used to the light. "And stop saying her and she. Tiny is a boy cat."

"I thought you said he was tiny," Zeke said.

"Well, he was when I named him. But he eats a lot. When I put out food, he finishes it, and then when I put out more, he finishes that too, and it takes a long time before he stops eating."

This was one fat cat. When he started walking in slow circles around Sly, and then over to check out Zeke and me, his stomach almost touched the driveway's asphalt. The stomach swung back and forth as he walked.

"What about the swinging stomach?" I said. "Is that a good trick?"

"Only if you could sort of set it swinging to music or something. But maybe . . . I mean that is really a hugely fat little cat."

Tiny put his paws on Zeke's skateboard and lowered the front of his body to stretch.

"I think he wants to ride your skateboard," Sly said.

Zeke smiled. "Now you're talking!"

He got off his board and went to pick up the cat — his arms stretched out straight in front of him, like the cat had cooties or something. "You don't pick up a cat like that!" Sly yelled. She rushed over and took Tiny from him.

She tried placing him on the board, but he walked right off. She did it again, and the cat just kept leaving. It was as though Tiny had met Zeke before and knew nothing good could come of this. Headline: CATASTROPHE AVOIDED IN CLAY COVES. No matter how many lives Tiny might have had, I wasn't sure any should be trusted to Zeke.

"What if we start with you sitting on the board with the cat on your lap, to get him used to it. Would that work?" Zeke asked.

"I'll try," Sly said.

"And I'll shoot for practice," Zeke said, pulling out Dad's reject camera.

"I'll just stand at the bottom of the driveway and make sure no cars are coming," I said.

"Oh, she's not going to ride all the way down there. Just a few feet, from the garage, maybe like not even a third of the way down. To get the cat, you know, used to it," he said, as though he'd been doing this kind of thing his whole life. Putting little girls and obese cats on skateboards and sending them down a sloping driveway. Sure. Just a third of the way. To get them used to it. Of course.

"Go hold the board for her, then hand her the cat."

Great. I was the assistant. I helped the director and the talent.

"How is she supposed to stop?" I asked.

"She puts out her feet. That'll stop the board."

"I think she should try without the cat the first time," I said.

"It wouldn't exactly be *That'sPETacular* material without a cat, moron," Zeke said.

Boy, were we having fun. "I meant so she learns how to stop. Moron."

"You guys are fun," Sly said. She smiled, and it seemed like she actually meant it.

I held the board with my feet while the cat was in my arms. "Go slow," I told her, trying to imagine how I'd explain the blood to her grandmother and mother after Sly capsized into a face-plant on the asphalt. I had a quick thought about helmets, but before I could even mention it, she was off.

"So like this?" she asked, and did it perfectly.

"No!" Zeke yelled. "Not at all like that! Did you hear me yell 'Action!'? I don't think you did because I didn't. That's only the most important part of this whole production. Nobody moves until I say so."

Sly rolled her eyes at me.

I'd never wanted a little sister. Ever. And in books, I wished I could just remove the pesky little sister who got in the big brother's way. I still got annoyed when I thought about some of them, like that Annie in those Magic Tree House books—she always made me want to scream, the way Jack would be figuring things out and Annie would screw everything up. But there was something appealing about having a sidekick when Zeke was at his worst—someone to roll eyes at me.

"AND! ACTION!" Zeke said.

Sly, sitting on the skateboard, rolled down the slope of the driveway about a third of the way, then put her feet down and stopped. "Ta-da!" she said.

"And CUT!" Zeke said. "Excuse me. Who gave you lines?"

"I don't know what you're asking me," Sly said. She looked at me. "I don't know what he's saying."

"'Ta-da,'" Zeke said. "That's what you said. No one told you to say anything. I'm the director."

"You know what this is?" Sly asked, standing up and reaching for her cat. "This is so not fun. Goodbye."

"No, no, no, no, no!" Zeke said. "I'm sorry. You can say *ta-da*. It's just my first time directing, and this camera is a little messed up, which takes some of my concentration away, and if you, as one of the stars of this film, felt *ta-da* was an important part, then I should consider that. I'll tell you what, practice now with the cat on your lap one time, okay?"

Sly looked unconvinced. She looked at me, and I shrugged, like it was her call.

"Maybe another day," she said. "I want to go inside now. And *you*," she said to Zeke, "need to be nicer. If you are, you can come back."

I'd been waiting my whole life for someone to say that!

"Where did I go wrong?" Zeke asked, probably not really expecting an answer, as Sly headed back into her house.

"Next time," I said, "try to suck less."

He gave me a look that suggested maybe I wasn't being what Dad would call my best self.

"You know what that was?" I asked Zeke as we headed slowly back to BTP.

"A total waste of time?"

"That," I said, "was PETacular."

Bush League

WE'D gotten to the point at home where we were eating cereal for almost every meal, and I really didn't want to live through another week like that, so I asked Pop to cover for Dad while I dragged Dad to the Shop A Lot.

I'm not sure why I picked that time to bring it up. Maybe it just felt too big to hold in anymore. "You know that student MacSophal?" I said. "The one you talk to a lot?"

"Patrick," my father said.

"It's not Patrick, right?" I had to be careful here. I definitely knew it was wrong to eavesdrop, and that was how I had gotten all my information.

"What are you talking about?" Dad asked, eyes on the road. "Patrick MacSophal, Group H."

"Well, that's sort of a weird last name, right?"

"I don't know. Is it?"

"Zeke and I think MacSophal is actually J-Mac, that steroid pitcher."

"And how did you come up with that?"

"I guess it was really Zeke who figured it out."

"Did you tell anybody else?"

"Who would we tell?" Did Dad picture our friends at school as some big, connected posse? Our world was a small world, after all. And anyway, I hadn't even shared the confirmation with Zeke. "So can you help me understand why you're letting a drug-using, steroid ex-athlete attend BTP? The guy was practically thrown out of Major League Baseball—"

"Casey, what are you talking about? He wasn't thrown out. He left."

"After Rhodes told everyone that MacSophal was the one giving him drugs."

"All he was guilty of is being accused of something. How come you're so fast to say he's guilty?"

"How come you're so fast not to?" I said. Everyone knew that J-Mac left baseball because he was caught red-handed. You didn't need to overhear his confession to Dad to know. He disappeared like a coward because he was ashamed.

"Well, we're here," Dad said.

It felt ridiculous to even consider getting out of the

car and pushing a giant shopping cart around, filling it with food. This conversation was too important. I turned to face him.

"I don't get it. If you knew it was him, why would you let him come to your school? He's a cheater. Taking drugs and giving them to other people isn't only breaking the law, it's cheating. It's giving yourself an unfair advantage over your teammates. It seems pretty obvious that he's guilty. So I don't understand why you would let a bad guy like that anywhere near the school. You always talk about integrity. What kind of integrity does J-Mac have? He's the anti-integrity."

"Casey. Whoa. You weren't there. You don't know what happened. How do you know who's guilty and who's innocent? Doesn't a journalist need to listen to all sides of the story and present it honestly and fairly?"

"An innocent guy doesn't disappear. He clears his name," I said. "I don't get why you're defending this jerk."

"Because everyone deserves a second chance," he said.

We got out of the car and slammed our doors. "And you need to call your mother again."

Unreal.

Digging in at the Plate

FROM Saturday evening until Monday morning, BTP students were on their own. Clay Coves was only ten minutes from great beaches, and a surprising number of umpire wannabes were also surfers. Some headed out for an afternoon surf after Saturday class was over. I always liked watching them return, standing on top of their cars and vans to take their boards down, stamping sand off their feet. They looked like some combination of human seals and penguins in their wetsuits.

This Saturday, a lot of guys went to the Tavern or the Well and drank too much and talked too loud when they came back to the dorms. Dad and Pop didn't like it. They said umpires need to command respect on and off the field.

But students worked so hard all week. I thought they deserved to relax however they wanted.

My brain was doing that thing again—thinking about everything from surfing umpires to the BTP schedule. Everything but the article I was sitting outside trying to start.

I reached into my pocket and pulled out my cell phone and Steamboat's number, but it just kept ringing and never went to voicemail. I ran back into the house and grabbed that folder Mrs. G. had given me and a BTP sweatshirt before I went back to where I'd been sitting. I looked through the folder, expecting to see maybe another number or an address. I had assumed that folder would have all the information I needed to run You Suck, Ump! Day. But all it had were receipts from the copy shop for each year's flyers. Nothing else.

"Did you decide what to write about?" It took me a minute, squinting through sun, to see that it was Soupcan.

"I need to turn something in on Monday," I said, putting the folder down.

"Monday like the day that is tomorrow?"

I had half a day. I nodded slowly. I already knew, kind of, what I was going to write, but my conscience was keeping me from starting.

Soupcan spotted a group of students walking

toward us. "How you doing?" he called. It was June Sponato, one of the Franklins (I still couldn't tell Robbie and Bob apart), two short guys, and MacSophal.

"What're you up to this evening?" Soupcan asked. "You all know Casey, right?" He pulled something—a lollipop—out of his back pocket and unwrapped it, then stuck it in his mouth.

They nodded at me. June Sponato smiled.

I smiled back at her, but had a hard time looking at MacSophal. Who did he think he was, telling my dad it would be fine to leave me? To go to Florida without me. Why didn't Dad talk about taking me? And who was this idiot cheater guy to tell my dad it was okay for a dad to leave his kid for five weeks anyway? It was annoying that I only knew this stuff because I'd listened to something I wasn't meant to hear, but it wasn't like I could unhear it now.

"Thinking about heading into town for some burgers," the Franklin said. "You want to come?" he asked Soupcan.

"May as well. Good luck with that, Casey. Let me know how it goes."

"Thanks," I said. "Oh, hey. Do you know how I can get in touch with Steamboat?"

"Sorry, man." They all walked toward the parking lot.

I put on my sweatshirt—even with the sun still out, a chilly hint of fall was in the air.

I wondered if I could really write the article I wanted to write. It was exciting to think about being the writer who solved one of baseball's big mysteries—what had happened to J-Mac? Even if the story did fall into my lap, I was still going to be the one to break it wide open. This could be really big. I could tell the world, or at least the middle-school students of Clay Coves, that the accused steroid user, the big-bearded wonder who never cleared his name, was now trying to start over right here in our town. That the former mega-bucks relief pitcher was now a lowly umpire-school student, fighting it out to get a shot at the Professional Umpire Evaluation Course in Cocoa.

Except.

I was pretty sure this fell under the category of Things You Know You're Not Supposed to Do Even Though No One Ever Exactly Told You. Other things on that list probably included putting beans up your nose and painting your guinea pig with honey.

I could ask Dad if it was okay to write about one of his students. But I knew he'd say no, not without MacSophal's permission, anyway.

So I could *not* ask and not give him a chance to

say no. And learn to live with a little guilt. Maybe Dad would never even know. Maybe I'd just start writing, and it wouldn't be good, and I wouldn't even have a whole stupid conflict on my hands.

I wrote my headline: BASEBALL'S MYSTERY MAN SPOTTED IN CLAY COVES, with the subhead What Happened to That Big-Headed Cheater?

I started writing, getting more and more keyed up as I went on. This could be the hugest article ever. Not only the kind that makes them publish a sixth-grader's piece for the first time. But the kind that some other kid might read, next year or years from now, and think, *Wow. A kid wrote this? A kid wrote this huge breaking-news story that won the Honorbound Competition?* He'd look at the byline and see *by Casey Snowden.*

I went back inside and got online to research J-Mac's career and his mysterious disappearance. It hadn't been in the news much lately, since it happened years ago, but back then, wow. It was a really big story. And then for a while afterward, there had been all these photo-only pieces about J-Mac sightings — in Tampa, at CitiField in New York. I guessed these days maybe people had stopped wondering. That was how it was with news. But what would happen if I really got this totally out-of-nowhere scoop, reminded people about

J-Mac, told the true, breaking-news story . . . that Mac-Sophal was really here, in Clay Coves, New Jersey, trying to become an umpire in the sport he ran away from. A rule breaker was studying the rules of baseball. It was too much!

There was so much to think about—right and wrong, exciting and scary—but instead of thinking, I just wrote.

Small Ball

WHEN I got on the bus, all I was thinking about was handing my article in after school. It was a lot better than thinking about Dad shipping me off to Mrs. Bob the Baker, and if I'd learned anything in the past few years, it was how not to think about her.

I was so excited about this article. I had worked really hard on it. I kind of couldn't wait to see everyone's reaction. I, Casey Snowden, was going to be the one who solved the mystery of baseball's great disappearance, the accused steroid user who fell off the face of the earth. Uncovered. By me!

I wouldn't be able to stay for the newspaper meeting after school today — I had to figure out how to get ready for You Suck, Ump! Day, how to get in touch with Steamboat — so I was planning to give the article to Mr. Donovan in English. I wondered if he'd be annoyed with me for not accepting the unwritten rule about sixth-graders, or if he'd maybe think it was cool that I was challenging it.

I had a hard time staying focused all day, even during English. At the end of the class, I took my time packing up my stuff, and I said, "Mr. Donovan?"

"Will I see you at the meeting later?"

"I can't," I said, standing up from my desk. "It's a really busy week at home, at the school, at Behind the Plate. You Suck, Ump! Day is coming up, and this year I'm kind of running the whole thing myself, so I need a ton of time to get ready."

He nodded.

"And I know this is weird, and that it's sort of a little against the rules, or the unwritten rules, but I don't agree with the rules, so I figured, well, I wrote an article, and I was hoping you could look it over. I won't be there to hand it in myself, so —"

"You really can't be there or you don't want to be there?" Mr. Donovan asked.

"I really can't. I mean, you're right that I don't exactly want to see Chris Sykes's face when I say I wrote an article, or listen to him, or whatever, but I really can't be there today." I almost said, "You could call my father if you don't believe me," but then I remembered I was twelve. Not six.

"I'll read it," he said.

✳✳✳

At home, Zeke and I sat down with pretzels and milk, a disgusting combination that he ate and drank all the time and which, to my own horror, I was starting to like too. As soon as we were done, I went to ask Mrs. G. if she had any other contact info for Steamboat.

She didn't.

"Okay, so his first name was Kelly. I know that. Do you at least know his last name?"

She didn't even go to a file drawer or anything. She just said, "Um," and looked at me. "Kelly? Really? I only knew him as Steamboat. And because his family was in Rhode Island, he didn't have a local bank account. So, Rhode Island, that's something, right? Or wait. It might have been Vermont. Or possibly Maine."

"Really? All I have to go on is the name Kelly, in the Northeast?" Perfect.

So Zeke and I went back to the kitchen, got more pretzels and more milk, and tried to think of everything we could having to do with You Suck, Ump! Day, from the flyers we needed to put up all over town, to letting people know when it was, to what time we needed to start, to what we needed to do to get the fields, stands, and public areas ready. It was a lot. I was pretty sure we could do it.

***

Zeke had to go home right away to "get some important stuff out in the mail." I wished him good luck with that, because his room was an organized person's nightmare — DVDs, addressed envelopes, stamps, postcards, reality TV contest entries — everything everywhere. I had no idea if half his ideas or entries or whatever were ever even submitted or if they were still in various layers on his bedroom floor, maybe to be discovered by some research scientists years from now, who would try to understand the deep meaning behind the video cards and entry forms addressed to *So You Think You're the Biggest Idiot?*

***

I went outside and made my way to the batting cages. I stopped in the space between two cages to watch Jorge Washington run through his calls. Bobbybo was there too, shaking his head (he didn't hide his disgust very well). "Look at your feet," he said to Jorge. It was bad news if you had to be told to look at your feet this late in the game.

"Right, right," Jorge said. I stepped a bit farther

into the cage and watched as he separated his feet more, shifted one a little ahead of the other. He got down into the crouch. His balance looked wobbly, and he flinched each time the pitching machine sent a ball into the catcher's glove. He was good at the rest of it, though: coming up to standing position, moving his right arm at a 90-degree angle with a single knocking motion, and calling a big, loud "Strike!" Then he got back into the crouch with his feet in the wrong position again.

I pushed tarp after tarp back, walking past the other cages until I spotted Dad and J-Mac talking outside, near the door and thought, *Wow, look at that — I don't even call him MacSophal anymore. He's J-Mac.* And at that very moment, I tripped over an Ibbit stick. I fell straight to the ground and looked around, relieved no one had seen. From the dark inside the cages, Dad and J-Mac looked like they were in a movie or onstage in a play — two big well-lit actors. I scooted closer and tried to hear what they were saying, but I couldn't make out a word. Until they were done, when J-Mac, walking away, turned back to yell, "Yeah, give him a call. Maybe you could start this January."

Start what in January?

January was when the Florida schools held their sessions.

What was with this guy, working so hard to get my dad to move BTP's Academy to Florida? I had to figure out how to stop this. Which would be doubly hard since I wasn't even supposed to know about it.

And Here's the Pitch

WORRY and excitement were fighting it out in my head. And my stomach. I was able to forget about the whole Florida nightmare, though, for nice patches of relief, when my excitement about the article would fill in that place. I couldn't wait to hear what Mr. Donovan had to say about what I wrote. I knew sports stories were always in the back of newspapers, but I wondered if maybe mine could end up on the front page because it was so much bigger than just another sports story.

I didn't know what Dad would think about me writing about one of his students without asking first, but journalists probably didn't ask their parents for permission, right? And what kind of rights was a cheater entitled to anyway?

Could this lead to a whole paparazzi kind of thing, with reporters all over the place, trying to get their own pictures and access to J-Mac? Even if that happened, wouldn't it be good for BTP, in a way? Maybe the wrong way, but still, in a way?

It was complicated.

***

At lunch, Zeke asked why I was so squirmy. He hardly ever noticed anything, so I guess I must have been pretty bad. But instead of telling him about my article or J-Mac, the reasons I was squirming, I looked at what he had brought—a squished banana and a pack of Oreos. That was all.

"Okay. Tell me again why you don't just buy lunch."

"With what money?" Zeke asked. Andrew deFausto reached to take one of the Oreos, but Zeke swatted him away before he could get it.

"I know your parents have money, Zeke. They'd pay for your lunches."

He nodded. "Yeah, they do."

Sense. All I wanted was for him to make some sense.

"How do you think I pay for the entry fees and postage and everything on all my entries?" he asked.

"I use my lunch money. And then I find things around the house I can eat at lunch."

"Do you want half?" I asked, unpacking my sandwich.

He nodded. And looked grateful. Maybe I could talk to Chet about making two lunches.

***

I waited and squirmed and nearly exploded through English, and then Mr. Donovan told me he hadn't had a chance to read my article but that he'd speak to me after class tomorrow.

Sure. I'd just wait another day. Because waiting was really easy for me.

When we got home from school, I needed some BTP time, so we went straight to the fields. Today they were working on stillness. When you call balls and strikes, you have to keep your head from moving. If your head moves at all, you change the angle you are viewing from, and it messes up your ability to see the line of the ball.

Before we even saw a whole group's rotation through the drill, Mrs. G. called Zeke and me into her office. "Okay. I have the flyers here," she said. "You better get them out today. And on your way out, Baby, please give these to your father." She handed me two phone-message slips. "I'm leaving early. Dana's picking up Sylvia, and I have a doctor's appointment. I can't be late."

All I really wanted to do was sit in the stands and watch some doofy students learn how to stop their heads from bobbing around while they crouched behind the plate, but there was no way I was going to mess up You Suck, Ump! Day. I went out to the garage and got my bike.

I took a quick look at the phone messages crumpled in my hand. The first one was from Clay Coves Community College, about setting up an umpire workshop for early next year. The other one was from the Phillies, and the message was "about spring training fields/January."

The Phillies' spring training fields were in Clearwater, Florida.

This was bad.

"Are you coming?" Zeke asked, pushing his skateboard onto my foot. He held up the camera and started recording me reading the phone message while kicking away his board.

"Turn that off," I said, annoyed. We put on our helmets and started to ride back toward Dad and the fields.

I couldn't believe this. Would Dad really have

made a decision like this without telling me? I couldn't move to Florida for five weeks and miss all that school. Or maybe I could! How cool would that be? But no, he'd never let me do that.

I wondered if it was already final: if he'd spoken to Mrs. Bob the Baker and now she was trying to get me used to her again so I could stay with her while Dad was in Florida.

But maybe it wasn't final.

And maybe if he never got the message, he'd never seal the deal.

"Let's just go downtown," I said to Zeke, leading him into a wide U-turn and shoving the messages deep into my pocket.

✳ ✳ ✳

We went to the library first. Zeke opened the door and said in a ridiculously loud voice, "Where do we put it, Case?"

I *shhhhhhhhhhhh*ed him. Had he never been in a library? Never, say, heard that you were supposed to lower your voice a little when entering the library? I walked over to the main desk, pulled one of the rolled-up flyers out of my backpack, and said, "Excuse me. I was wondering where I could post a sign about a community event?"

"Nice," Zeke said. Loudly.

"What kind of community event?" the woman asked.

"It's at my dad's school, and it's free, and —"

"We only post events of cultural significance," she said, pushing glasses up on her nose.

Without a second of hesitation, Zeke said, "It's kind of like theater. And there's limited seating. And we wanted to be sure library patrons were aware of this opportunity."

Library patrons?

"May I see your sign?" the woman asked.

I reached into my backpack and handed it over.

"Behind the Plate?" she asked, a real question in her voice. I thought everyone in town had heard of our school.

"That's the production company," Zeke said. "Do we put it on that board behind that rack?" he asked, taking it back before she could read NO PRODUCE ALLOWED. Or get to the word *suck*.

"That will be fine," she said.

"You're good," I said to him as we walked away.

"Tell me something I don't know."

✳ ✳ ✳

From there, we went to Crossroads Deli, Book Cove, Town Hardware, Clay Coves Cones, Cove Coffee, and Angelo's Pizza, hanging flyers all over town. In Angelo's, when I was reaching into my backpack, I came upon the ad sales folder for the school newspaper. I asked, "Has anyone tried to sell you an ad in the school paper, Angelo?"

He rubbed his white-flour hands together. "Not this year, I don't think. Unless — Maria?" He called into the back for his wife. "You buy some ad in the paper this year? Casey's here collecting."

Zeke looked at me, like, *What the* —? and I said, "No, no, Angelo. I'm not collecting. I was wondering if you wanted to buy one. But never mind. Why should you buy one?"

"That," Zeke said, "is your sales pitch?"

"I should buy one because then students will come here to eat their pizza instead of going to 4-C Pizza. What's it cost?"

I handed him the form. "Can I get a slice?" I asked.

"Me too," Zeke said.

"Two slice," Angelo said. I loved that. Two slice.

The door opened and in walked Ralphie-O, the guy who cut the grass at BTP. "Casey, Casey, Casey at the bat. What are you doing here?"

"Tearing my husband from his money," Maria said, bringing tubs of pizza dough to the front counter and setting them down with a loud thump that sent flour puffing up in a small cloud.

"Robbing the joint, Casey?"

"I'm sorry," I said, mortified by the whole stupid ad-selling thing. "I'll just take my pizza when it's ready." I dragged my backpack to a booth and sat down. My legs were a crazy kind of tired—I couldn't imagine ever standing again.

"Casey's selling ads," Angelo said. "For that newspaper at the school."

"So you're a salesman now, huh? I always figured you'd be an umpire!"

All I wanted was to be a reporter, but for now, Ralphie-O was right: According to the rules, I could only be a salesman. And then, on cue, my brain started bumping up against the excitement of tomorrow and talking about my article with Mr. Donovan. How I'd found this amazing story that no one even realized was right here in our town. Wait. Everyone was looking at me. "Not really, no." I said. "We came to ask Angelo if he'd let us hang this flyer for You Suck, Ump! Day."

"But what's this here?" Ralphie-O took the ad folder from Angelo and looked it over. "I'm going to take an ad, Casey. For my landscape service."

"Cool," I said. "Thanks."

"Me too," Angelo said. "Let me get the checkbook."

The Game's on the Line

WE left Angelo's with two full stomachs and two ads sold, but we were both too tired to start riding back home. We crossed the street to the park where some kids in Clay Coves Fall Ball shirts were practicing. They were probably nine or ten. I liked the way they had major-league attitude and moves, kind of like they were swaggering, even if their actual skills weren't all that great yet. One of them did a perfect imitation of Jackson Alter's stance, the way he held up his hand to the ump to indicate he wasn't ready yet, a kind of wiggle in his hips as he took short practice swings.

It reminded me of my Little League days. Tee ball was supposed to be fun, but it made me crazy how wrong the rules were. Like everyone batted each inning, no matter how many outs there were. And there were, like, fifteen people playing the field. What sport is that? Still, it was fun to be on a team, to wear a uniform, to go out for ice cream after the game.

But by the time I was in third grade, playing baseball was already . . . I don't even know what to call it. Lots of fathers cared way too much about having good players on their teams, and coaches always let their kids play better positions than anyone else, and parents even argued with the umpires. It was about the least fun thing in the world. The year Mrs. Bob the Baker left, I quit playing baseball and started writing about it. A lot of my friends quit around the same time. Charley Haddon's the only kid I know who still plays. His dad coaches.

I reached into my pocket and felt those crumpled messages shoved down deep. That led me back to J-Mac's conversations with my dad and the growing seed of knowledge that my dad was moving BTP's Umpire Academy to Florida. Which left no place for me. Except maybe with Mrs. Bob the Baker, and really, it might not have sounded like it, but that was the end of the world, right there. So I shoved the thought away.

"You're a little green, Casey. You okay?"

I had not lived a life full of secrets. I was a pretty honest guy. I wanted to tell Zeke about the article, but I wasn't sure I could trust him with the confirmation that J-Mac was right here, a student at BTP. He'd find some way to turn it into a reality-TV something or other, or sell a photo to one of those celebrity newspapers. I also wanted to tell him how worried I was that my dad was going to move. That one was easier, so I started talking. I meant to tell him everything, but I spent so long on the I-can't-let-my-dad-take-Umpire-Academy-to-Florida-every-year part that we never really got to J-Mac. I would, though.

But now I had made him upset. "What makes you think Ibbit won't find a way to take you with him?"

"Why else would he suddenly be so interested in how often I talk to my mother, and why would she suddenly decide that we need to get back to scheduled visits and all that? The plan's already in motion. They only forgot one part — telling me."

"But your mom lives almost an hour away, right? How would you get to school?"

"I have no idea," I said. "Maybe she'd drive me? Or send me with her loser husband? Or maybe I'd have to go to the school near her for those weeks? I have no idea."

"But it would be awful if they didn't do Academy here. I love the before-and-after videos. It was my idea, and I wanted to always be the one who does them, and—"

"And also you want your best friend to be nearby? Do you realize I'd have to stay with my mother the whole time Dad's gone, which is bad enough—no, worse than that—but also means not near you?"

"We have to stop this," he said.

"I know. But I have no idea how."

Zeke was silent an unusually long time (silence not being his strong suit), and then we both stood up and started riding toward home.

Until we saw a little girl. A little girl with long black hair. Sitting alone on the steps in front of St. Luke's and wiping her eyes.

I ditched my bike by the curb and walked over. "You okay?"

Sly nodded. "Hi, Casey. Oh, and you too. Hello, you," she said to Zeke.

"What's going on?" I asked.

She looked out to the street, then said, "Nothing. Just sitting."

"By yourself?"

She nodded.

"Okay," Zeke said, still on his skateboard. "Have a good one."

I shot him a look. "Did you miss your bus or something?" I asked.

"I had Brownies," she said, like that answered everything.

"So where are the other Brownies?" I sat next to her.

"Home. Not my home. Their homes. They all went home."

"And . . . no one noticed you were sitting here by yourself?"

She started to squirm a little. And then she said, "They said if my mother forgot to pick me up one more time, I couldn't come to more meetings, so I told them she was here. And I hid behind that bush to wait for her. And then everyone left. And she hasn't got here yet."

"Come on, Casey. Let's go," Zeke said.

"Why don't you come with us? We'll take you home," I said.

"No, I better wait here," Sly said, not moving.

"Well, me and Zeke were going to come look for you, so this would just save us some time. We were saying how we wanted to try again to shoot some video of you and Tiny, if you think that would be okay. Maybe we could all go to your house and —"

"We were not—" Zeke started, until I gave him a look. Then he hung his head like a bad dog.

Sly stood up. "I guess that would be okay."

✳✳✳

We headed to her house, with Zeke on his skateboard and me pushing my bike. Once we got there, Sly entered a code that opened the garage. Before long, she came out with the same box. She walked over to Zeke and said, "I hope you're in a better mood today."

"This won't take long," Zeke said, a not-answer if I ever heard one.

Down the street, we could hear someone mowing a lawn.

"So what are we doing today?" she asked.

"I'm not sure," Zeke said, "but it won't take long. Let's see what happens when we put the cat on the board. Maybe he got used to it last time."

I brought the skateboard to the top of the driveway. Sly carried the box over and pulled out Tiny. She put him on the skateboard, and he walked right off with that sort of snotty attitude cats sometimes have.

"All right, then," Zeke said, after Sly had tried it a few more times, "let's just pick up where we left off last time. Sly, you're going to sit with the cat on your lap until we can get him used to the feel of the board. But instead of your lap, why don't you let part of him touch the board itself, like sitting between your legs or something."

"I can hold the board," I said.

"No, that's okay," Sly said, sitting on it with her legs holding her in position. "I've got it."

"So what do I do?"

Zeke shrugged.

I walked to the bottom of the driveway, where it met the street, and examined my shoelaces. They were filthy. And tearing. But I was grateful to have a chance to sit down and rest my worn-out-from-going-all-over-Clay-Coves muscles.

Zeke and Sly were bickering about who was supposed to say what, and I was trying to tune them out when finally, that noise, that lawn-mower noise, stopped. I looked down the block and saw a bunch of guys putting some equipment in the back of a truck and recognized it as Ralphie-O's truck. Ralphie-O himself rolled one of those big riding lawn mowers onto the back.

I shifted my focus back to my shoelace, then watched Zeke and the cat and Sly for a while as they tried to figure out what they were doing. That was when a lot of things happened at once. Ralphie-O started driving down the street. I looked up to wave and out of the corner of my eye, saw a fast, furious skateboard, with at least one girl, and possibly a cat, heading into the street, right into the path of the truck. I must have jumped up and sort of thrown my body on top of the skateboard to stop it, to turn it, to keep it from rolling directly in front of the truck. And somehow, I don't know if it was with my hands or my body, my feet, or what, but nothing bad happened.

Well, no one got badly hurt. The truck braked, an awful, loud *screeeeeeeeeech*, another car pulled over to the side of the road, stopped suddenly, and the driver jumped out, and there I was in the street, near the curb, with a girl with two bloody knees, a skateboard, and a cat racing back toward the house, its stomach skimming the ground, swaying back and forth.

It was hard to not explode during all of this. My heart was beating too fast, and I kept looking at where the truck had stopped, where the skateboard had stopped, and thinking how it could have . . . how Sly could have . . .

Sly didn't even cry. She stood right up, watched the cat safely reach the garage, then bent over and looked at her knees, just curious, though. Not freaking out.

I couldn't even think thoughts in the right order. It was just this big jumble of my racing heart and my guilt about being the whole reason we were here, putting her on a skateboard, and I wanted to disappear right that minute, or go back in time and think of another way to talk Sly off the front steps of St. Luke's.

But all at once, everyone was around me — the woman who had jumped out of that car, who had to be Sly's mother, Ralphie-O, and some guys who worked for him. Everyone was asking everyone else, "What happened? Are you okay? Is the little girl okay?"

Sly's mother went inside for something to clean Sly's knees, and Sly stood next to me, clutching my arm. I wanted to clutch someone's arm too! I wanted someone to tell me it was okay, even though I kind of mostly knew it was. I looked around for Zeke. He was sitting by himself on the grass near the driveway, where he'd been filming. I was relieved that he was no longer filming, even though I thought that if he had turned that camera on himself, he might have had a perfect entry for *So You Think You're the Biggest Idiot?*

"Listen, are you okay?" I asked.

Sly kept shaking her head and saying, "It's just like that," which seemed kind of crazy, which is not exactly the way you want someone to be acting after an accident that was kind of your fault.

"Is she okay?" Ralphie-O asked me, as though she had just been speaking to me in kid code that I would obviously be able to translate.

I shrugged. How was I supposed to know? I wasn't

even sure I was okay. My heart was still speed-beating, like it was trying to find its way right out of my chest.

"You saved my life," she said. "Just like Larry the Lifeguard saved Patrick and SpongeBob."

"Are you okay, Sly?" I asked again. "Why don't you go inside and—"

"I'm fine. I hurt my knees, but I'm fine. But did you hear me?"

"Go inside—"

"Isn't that the coolest thing, that you're like Larry? Like a hero, Casey. But wait, does that make me Sponge-Bob or Patrick?"

She didn't know Zeke as well as I did. "I think Zeke must be Patrick. You can be SpongeBob. Are you okay with that?"

"Definitely."

We *were* talking in kid code!

Ralphie-O looked around and said, "So, Casey, maybe make up your mind, you know? You're going to be an umpire, a salesman, or a hero? Man alive, that was a good heads-up play."

"Thanks."

Sly's mother, back now with washcloths and bandages, said to Ralphie-O, "Thanks for stopping and making sure she was okay." And then to Sly she said, "Are you sure you're okay, Sylvia?"

But Sly was still talking to me, as though nobody else had said anything. "So you saved my life. That's a big deal. Can I do a favor for you now, to even stuff out?"

"You don't have to."

"I want to. Maybe I could help you at your school or something."

Sly's mom said, "Sylvia, come inside now. Let's go." Then she turned to me, and as I was ready for her to thank me for helping her daughter, she asked, "Why were you letting my kid play in the street? Shouldn't you know better than that?"

I was trying to stammer my way through an answer—like, *Lady, no. I saved her from the street. And brought her home when you forgot her.* But she turned and started walking with Sly, who was limping back up the driveway. When Sly passed Zeke, he asked, "Want to film just one more time? We were so close."

"This really isn't that much fun," she said. "I don't want to do it anymore." And then she went inside.

I looked at Zeke. He said, "Don't say a word."

All Bases Covered

THE next morning on the bus, Zeke literally ran up the steps and to our seat. He sat next to me. In fact, he again sort of sat on top of me, but then shifted over. "I know I've said this before, but you won't believe this. Really. You won't."

"Okay," I said. I was barely holding in all my own news.

"Remember that contest?" He didn't wait for an answer. "Remember? Where you have to come up with your own reality TV show idea—Your Show Here?"

I started to get a really bad feeling. That near-catastrophe yesterday had kept me awake most of the night, so I was twitchy to begin with.

"You had to send in your idea by filling out this online form, and I did and then I forgot about it, mostly, while I was working on other things, but I got a response, an email this morning that mine was one of fifty ideas being considered."

"You won?"

"No, not yet. They're just considering it. But still!"

I asked slowly, because I was very, very scared. "What idea did you enter?"

"America's Next Umpire!"

I pictured the headline: OVERWEIGHT CATS OF NJ BREATHE SIGH OF RELIEF.

But wait, what?! "What are you talking about?"

"A TV show about Umpire Academy, and America gets to vote on who becomes the next umpire. They get to choose who gets sent to Cocoa."

I could think of so many reasons that was a bad idea. "What does America know about umpire training?" was the first to come out.

"The show will sort of educate them, right? Like they'll learn along with the students what the right stance is, how to, I don't know, crouch, all that stuff. Everything about timing, and knowing the rules, and positioning. You know how I filmed all that stuff for the before tapes? That's how I got the idea."

Part of me thought it was a bad idea, but who was I? Some punk kid who was maybe too close to umpire school. Some real live national contest-judging person obviously thought it was a good idea. Maybe Zeke had found his reality-TV claim to fame.

Zeke said, "I couldn't decide if it was okay to do this without checking with Ibbit. I figured if he said no, we'd just can it. But when you told me about Florida, I thought about how maybe if more people knew about the school, Ibbit wouldn't have to move Academy to Florida. Right? And I know if I ask, Ibbit will say no. But I know you don't want to stay with your mother, and who would even sit with me on the bus if—"

"I get it," I said. Who knows? Maybe Zeke's idea *could* somehow help the school. If more people heard about Academy, more people would enroll, and maybe if we got more people, like we used to have, it could always stay in New Jersey. Even if Zeke's idea didn't go the whole way through, maybe it could be featured on a finalist show, and people who never knew about Behind the Plate would hear about us. "Didn't you need my dad's permission or signature or something?"

"You don't need to sign any release forms until the next level," Zeke said as the bus pulled into the lot. "I have to send a video by next week, so I want to film on You Suck, Ump! Day. Which I planned to do anyway. Now I just have a better reason."

He stood to get off the bus and I blurted out, "You know that MacSophal dude?"

He nodded.

I whispered. "It's really him! I wrote an article about it, and I'm hoping they'll print it in the school paper."

Zeke's mouth was wide open. I had left him speechless.

I know!

Way Off Base

I TRIED to figure out what Mr. Donovan was going to say by looking at him. He didn't appear to be almost exploding with sure-to-win-the-Honorbound-Competition joy, but maybe he didn't want to be too obvious. Inside my stomach, this little seal of hope flipped back and forth. A dancing, prancing, ball-on-nose balancing seal performed slippery turns of nervousness each time I thought about what he was going to say to me. But even if he was blown away by my article, would Chris Sykes and the other editors be impressed enough to break that stupid rule? And then . . . what about Dad? He knew this was what I wanted more than anything. He'd have to be happy for me finally getting to do what I wanted, right?

At last, after we compared and contrasted the

themes of two boring short stories, the bell rang. I shot up to Mr. Donovan's desk.

"Thanks for staying, Casey," he said as the last student left the room. "I wanted to talk to you about your submission. I think it's super that you tried your hand at this. But you do realize that the paper has never published an article written by a sixth-grader, right?"

"Uh, yeah," I said. "I vaguely remember hearing something like that." I was sure he'd get to the but-we'll-make-an-exception-soon part, so I nodded and kept nodding, to keep him moving swiftly along.

He handed back my article.

Wait, what? He was handing back my article? "Did you even read it?"

"I did," he said.

"Are you saying it's not good enough, or that we can't break the rule?"

He stood from his desk and went to get his keys, which made me think he'd be out the door in a second. What was going on?

"It's not a bad article, Casey. There's a lot going on here, and I'm not sure where to start. As we go through more meetings, you'll have a chance to learn a lot — about objectivity, the ethics of journalism, invasion of privacy, interviews. That's a good starting point. Interviews. Given your access to this guy, I couldn't help but wonder where you got your information and why you didn't include an interview."

I couldn't talk. I was so stunned I literally could not speak. I had known exactly what Mr. Donovan was going to say, and it was very much not this.

"Honestly, Casey, I admire the effort you've put into this. I think it's great that a member of the Newspaper Club is writing, with the full knowledge that it will almost surely not be published. Any teacher would appreciate that kind of initiative. If you want to continue to grow from this, I recommend you interview this character. I think that would strengthen your piece considerably. I'd like to see you include that. And you have to work to keep your own feelings out of the article — you'll want to reconsider your headline, for example."

I wasn't even sure I was listening. "And then could it be included in the paper?"

"It's not up to me. I'm trying to help you write the strongest piece you can, help you learn. I'd be happy to talk more about this with you another time, but I have to meet someone for a quick lunch." Before he stepped out the door, he said, "Keep at it, Casey. You show a lot of promise."

Promise. Like potential.

Like not there yet.

Benched

ON the bus home, I was still reeling, and feeling grateful that Zeke had been picked up early for an orthodontist appointment — I could barely keep it together. I couldn't believe Mr. Donovan hadn't loved my article. He must not have been a big baseball fan. Anyone who knew anything about baseball would have loved that article.

Still, I kept thinking about what Soupcan said, how it's not always what you're writing about. Sometimes you could make someone love your article by the way you wrote it, even if, as a reader, you didn't care about that subject.

And I hadn't done that.

The truth was it wasn't good enough. I hadn't written a good enough article.

No one started out perfect, I knew that. But I'd

really thought I'd hit it out of the park. I'd been sure I'd nailed it. And in the end, all I did was prove that sixth-graders weren't good enough to write for the paper.

BTP students had to listen to their evaluations in the outfield, look their instructors in the eye, and hear all the ways they needed to improve. It was awkward—and I hated it—but it was also the reason they started to change from lamely going through the motions to looking like real umpires.

It killed me that my article wasn't perfect. I didn't want to need to learn. I wanted to see my byline in the first issue. I didn't want to think about what Mr. Donovan had said, that the article would be better with an interview. I hadn't included one because I hadn't wanted to. When I thought about the reason for that, I kept getting answers that seemed untrue. Like I was lying to me. Which was kind of a waste of time, since I was right there in my brain with the lies. More than anything, it was scary. And I had figured J-Mac would say no anyway. And I just kind of wanted to tell the story the way I knew it to be, without having to deal with what J-Mac had to say for himself.

And then there were those words Mr. Donovan used, *invasion of privacy*. That got me a little worried. I had thought reporters were supposed to sniff stories out. And expose the bad guys. Did reporters have to protect the privacy of cheaters?

I got off the bus and walked through the gate, up the long drive. I headed straight out to the rear field to watch Pop work students through his balk-or-not-a-balk drill. I sat on the top row of the bleachers. Mac-Sophal was in Pop's group today, and it was pretty clear that he was good at this. He had a great understanding of the game, he was quick, and he used his voice and body well. Pop would say that he sounded like he meant it.

I wasn't exactly hit by a lightning bolt, and I didn't see any giant cartoon lightbulbs appear above my head, but I did have that kind of sudden realization about my article: I had completely forgotten to be objective. Mr. Donovan pretty much said as much, but I had thought, I don't know, it somehow didn't apply to me. Or that all bets were off when you were writing about someone who was a known cheater. But anyone who read the article could see that I, the supposed-to-be-fair reporter, was happy that J-Mac had lost his place in the major leagues, and that I thought there was some kind of justice that he couldn't play anymore, that he couldn't even get a coaching job, that he was trying to get back to baseball on a back road, by attending the third-best umpire school in the country.

I had to rewrite it. And make it better. And think about an interview. He was, after all, right here. It was an opportunity too good to pass up. Wasn't it?

The thought of that byline—*by Casey Snowden*—kept my brain revving. This was no time to give up.

Called Up from the Minors

I TRIED rewriting that article every day. I made no progress. Unless you counted the false starts piling up in the recycling bin as progress. I decided to try again on Sunday, my day off from everything. I was planning to sleep late and write for the rest of the day.

And then I heard someone *kalump*ing up the stairs.

"Go away," I said when the door opened.

"Don't make me sing," Zeke said.

I put the pillow over my head and pulled the blanket up over it.

He started singing that I was his sunshine. His only sunshine. I made him happy. When skies were gray. "Ready to start your day?" he asked.

I let the silence answer that one. I couldn't be less ready.

"Let's go eat breakfast."

"Izzat Zeke?" I heard from Dad's room.

"Ow," I said, having literally kicked myself for forgetting to lock the doors last night.

"Good morning, Ibbit," Zeke called, all crazy-morning happy.

"Morning, Zeke."

***

When I got downstairs, all the cereal boxes were on the table, along with four bowls, and Zeke was sitting by himself, looking over the new notes I'd made for You Suck, Ump! Day.

"What's this about crowd control?" he asked.

"Remember the year we had too many people, and Joe Blevensky, the cop, came and threatened us?"

"Oh, yeah. Blevensky."

"We need someone at the gate to count, so that doesn't happen again. We need to turn away people after we get six hundred and forty. I checked with Mrs. G. That's the number."

"Okay," Zeke said. "I'll do that. I'll be like a bouncer. That'll be sick."

We stopped to pour cereal into our bowls. Zeke started eating but didn't let that keep him from talking.

"So you remember I'm recording the whole thing, right?"

"While you're working the front gate as bouncer?"

"Oh."

"Right."

"So you're saying I can't do two things at once."

"What we need is a staff," I said.

"Or a servant," Zeke said.

That's when I thought about Sly. And how she wanted to do something for me after I saved her skateboard from meeting Ralphie-O's truck. But more than that, I thought about how she was always asking for something to do, how she seemed to really want to be part of BTP.

"What about Sly?" I said.

"She's what, two?"

"I think she's eight, and yeah, that's young. But she's older than her age, kind of."

Zeke was making a face and shaking his head. "I can't see her being a bouncer."

"Yeah, I know. But I think we should find something for her to do this one time. Like maybe she could be the No-Produce Enforcer."

"We never had one of those before."

"So?"

"So we can do that?" Zeke asked.

"We are the kings. We can do anything."

We sat at that table until we had reviewed every single thing we needed to do for You Suck, Ump!

Day one more time. And then we headed back to Sly's house, me on my bike and Zeke on his skateboard.

"Go ring the bell," I said to Zeke. Sometimes I could trick him into things if he wasn't thinking.

"No way. You ring the bell."

We heard a loud sneeze from the front porch of the house, and then Sly's mother walked outside in her robe. If she was surprised to see two guys she didn't really know in her driveway, you'd never have known it.

"Good morning," she said. "You must be Sly's new friends."

I wanted to kick Zeke before he said anything stupid. I asked, "Is she around?"

She sneezed again. "She must be. Hey, would you mind bringing me that paper?"

Zeke ran down to the end of the driveway, grabbed the yellow-bagged newspaper, and ran it up to her.

"You're the one with the camera?"

"Zeke," he said.

"And you're Ibbit's son? The one that played in the street with Sylvia?"

I nodded. Then said, "Well, I'm his son, but actually, I was just trying to keep—"

"And you're filming something with the cat? Why are you doing that?"

"For fun," Zeke said.

"Not for TV?" she asked.

"Oh, well, yeah. I did want to try to get something onto *That'sPETacular*," he said. "But Tiny, well—"

"Okay," she said, interrupting. "But nothing dangerous today, guys, okay? Sylvia's not allowed to play in the street." And she stepped inside.

Zeke and I looked at each other, like *What was that?* "I kind of wanted to say to her, 'Yeah. We'll stay out of the street. And maybe you'll remember to pick her up after Brownies next time.'"

"You should have!" Zeke said. "She was acting like we were terrorists or something."

Sly's mom was a weird mix of protective and . . . whatever's the opposite of protective. Absent, maybe? I knew a lot about absent moms, but Sly's mom was kind of in a category all her own.

Just then, Sly came outside with her hands up, like she was showing us she wasn't holding Tiny's box. Or a weapon. "I told you I don't want to play that video thing anymore with Tiny."

"Yeah, I know," I said. "There's something else I wanted to ask you. Do you want to help us at Behind the Plate? You'd be totally in charge of an important part of security at a big, important day."

She just looked at me, silently, like she was waiting for the bad-news part. So I kept talking. "It's this sort of crazy day, and we need extra people to help, and I thought you'd be really good at helping us with this one thing."

She put her hand on her hip. "What one thing?"

"Produce control," I said.

"Yeah, I don't know what that means. What do I control?"

Zeke sighed—loudly, theatrically—then sighed again and sat down, like he had tons of important plans and we were keeping him from them. This kid who had dragged me out of bed when I was sleeping.

"We have this day when hundreds of people come to the school and watch the umpire students. And they yell at them too, but it's okay, because we want them to do that." I never realized, until I started explaining it out loud, how incredibly stupid You Suck, Ump! Day sounded. "Anyway, we need to make sure that no one brings in any fruit or vegetables to throw at the students, and I thought you could help us with that."

She gave me a look like she was waiting for me to say "Just kidding!" But I didn't, and so she said, "Wait a sec." She ran into the house, screaming, "Grandma! Grandma!"

"You sure this is a good idea?" Zeke asked. Honestly, I was shocked. He did so many things that were not good ideas that I hadn't even known the concept of *good idea* was one he was familiar with.

"Well," I said, "to quote every cartoon ever, 'What could possibly go wrong?'"

Sly came running back. "I can do it," she said. "I'm, like, totally in charge of the fruit, you said, right? Like I'm the fruit boss?"

"Yup."

She smiled. And then she saluted.

Playing Hardball

THE day before You Suck, Ump! Day was my favorite. Because it was when my dad was so not my dad.

Students were now all more confident than when they had arrived. The ones who could tell they were doing well were strutting a bit. The better students hung out together, and the not-so-good students stayed in their own groups.

Dad and Pop called all the students and staff out onto field one. Dad explained, kind of, what was going to happen over the next two days. But not completely. I never missed this speech. Even though it was one of those gray, heavy-air, humid days, the kind that usually make me move slowly, I ran home from the bus to make sure I was there in time.

"You guys have done a lot of great work out here so far," Dad said. "But these haven't been real baseball conditions, have they?"

He paused, but it was just to let them think. He wasn't waiting for an answer.

"Baseball's not a quiet game. When you're in a ballpark, there are people selling beer, there are loud and rowdy fans, there are managers unhappy with the calls you've made, there are hecklers screaming at you, there are players grumbling or eyeballing you for a called third strike. It is not a classroom setting.

"Over the next two days, you're going to get a taste of that. Today you'll mostly deal with playing-field situations. You'll see a little later on. And tomorrow, we invite some of our town's good people to fill these stands and, well, yell at you."

There was a laugh that sort of rippled through the students.

"Okay, let's break down into our assigned areas. Groups H and J, you're in the cages. The rest of you, those who were on field two, can head over there now with Soupcan and Pop."

Dad walked off the field and I followed. He went into the small office he had off a classroom and called out to Mrs. G., "Is it ready?" I noticed he hadn't shaved—that was part of the show . . . It helped him feel like a manager for some reason.

She brought in a Braves uniform and smiled. "I feel like this session just got started."

"Any calls?" Dad asked.

"Yes. There was one from someone with the Phillies about Florida? Something like that."

Dad sneaked a look at me and then nodded quickly at Mrs. G. He slipped the uniform over his clothes, then slowly walked back out to the field.

Before I could ask her, "What was that about Florida?" the phone rang, and she answered it. I followed Dad to the field.

Bobbybo was calling situations, and students in the plate ump and base ump positions were trying to remember everything they'd learned about what position they were supposed to be in, how to spot and call a balk, the infield fly rule . . . baseball is so complicated. And Dad was about to make it a million times worse for them.

"Ball," the student called, just like he'd been instructed to do.

"Whatzat?" Dad called out from the dugout in a weird, fake southern accent.

"I said ball," the student said, not looking at Dad. Just looking out at the mound.

"You called that strike a ball?"

"Quiet now," the student said. He sounded terrified.

Dad was near home plate now. The student looked a little freaked out. Who wouldn't, with a deranged-looking not-clean-shaven version of my dad, talking in a crazy southern accent and wearing a Braves uniform instead of his usual umpire blue?

"Listen," Dad said, "you're giving all the calls to the other team. I don't know if you've got something going on with them—" Here Dad stopped talking and poked his finger in the student's chest.

The student should have already thrown Dad out of the game. Instead he said, "I'm sorry. I thought it looked like a ball," sounding like he was about to cry.

"Whatzat, son?"

"I thought it was a ball." Seriously, about to cry.

Dad turned around to all the students watching. His body language changed at once. He was no longer a slouching, slow-talking, somewhat-deranged-looking manager. He was Ibbit. Instructor Ibbit. "That, boys and girls, is how not to be an umpire." He turned to the student and said, "I'm sorry you had to be the first one.

It's hard. But you need to work on conveying authority. And not letting a manager walk all over you. If you think this was hard, wait until the crowds are screaming at you tomorrow."

And how lucky he was, I thought, that Zeke and Sly and I would be on hand to protect him from having tomatoes hurled at his head.

Full Count

AFTER dinner I went outside with a notepad and pencil, and I waited. I was out of my comfort zone, but there are some things you can't prepare for.

I knew what I had to do.

I sat on the bench between the cafeteria and the dorms, trying to calm the sloshy feeling in my stomach. The night grew dark around me.

I heard steps on the path. "How's it going, Case?" Bobbybo lifted my baseball cap and slapped it back down. "I'm going to Clay Coves Cones. You wanna come?"

"No, thanks," I said. I actually did want ice cream — I always wanted ice cream — but I wanted what I was there waiting for even more.

I couldn't see much in the darkness, but I heard a

car door open and shut, Bobbybo's motor starting up. The wheels worked against the gravel in the lot until it grew quiet again. Just the buzz of New Jersey insects and the dim light of the moon.

More steps on the path, not him. Not him. Not him. Groups of people who weren't him. Not him. Lone guys strutted along who weren't him. Not him. Not him.

I thought about having to go back to Mr. Donovan without an interview. With one of the not-yet-exactly-great revisions I had written in my notebook. Maybe there were some old interviews online I hadn't found yet. Maybe if I looked harder, I'd find some good information I could use to make my article better. Did I really need an interview for this to work, just because Donovan said I did?

And then, finally, one more person, passing with a quick "Wassup?" MacSophal was about to walk right past me, back to the dorms.

This was it.

"Could I talk to you for a few minutes?" My voice was loud, maybe too loud.

In the darkness, I could make out the shrug of his too-big shoulders. "What's going on?"

One deep breath. "I was wondering if I could interview you." I'd been focusing on his shoulders, then his chest, but I shifted, looked him in the eye. It was dark, but we could see each other well enough.

"I don't think that would be such a good idea," he said, turning toward the dorms. As he started to walk away, there was a quick sound, and then a sudden shock of brightness. The field lights came on. Like something brought back to life, the bright summer green of the outfield grass shone where an instant earlier it had been dark. J-Mac turned. There was something about a diamond under the lights. It reminded you of what you loved about baseball. It stopped J-Mac right in his tracks.

"You're not just looking to interview some run-of-the-mill umpire-school student, right? This is about me? My life?"

"Yeah. For the school newspaper."

"What does your dad think about you interviewing me?"

I shrugged, since he didn't know anything about it at all. My dad had his secrets, and I had mine.

A motor started up and drowned out the sound of chirping insects. A lawn mower rolled out to center field. Ralphie-O sometimes came to mow the fields really late here, as BTP was his only client with night-time lighting.

J-Mac turned back to me. "Your dad's a really good

guy, Casey. I'll talk to you, but just for a little while, okay?" He sat down next to me on the bench. I could feel it shift from his weight and thought about how if it were a seesaw, I'd be flying up into the sky.

I took another deep breath. I wanted to start with the juicy part—the minute he heard that Reggie Rhodes had ratted him out. But I knew it would be a better strategy to get him talking about the good times. I asked, "What's your best memory of playing in the major leagues?"

He leaned back and rubbed the back of his neck, the start of a smile at the corners of his mouth. "The time I came in for the eighth inning in a tie game and mowed down three batters with nine pitches," he said. "Nine easy strikes. Or maybe the first time my parents saw me play at Wrigley. No, you know what the best was? When I realized I could throw this cutter. That it worked. This crazy pitch that most other guys couldn't throw. You should have seen the looks on coaches' faces when I had my stuff working, when the cutter had all that late movement."

I was taking notes as fast as I could, not wanting to miss one word of this.

"Have you ever seen a good cutter, Casey? It's a magic pitch. It's not a fastball. It's not a slider. When your cutter's working, you get guys chasing pitches. And when they *do* connect, they break their bats. One game, Brady Burnett broke three in a single at bat."

One story led to the next. I hoped he'd never stop.

"My first time in the show, first major league game, I faced two batters. And I walked each one. On four pitches each." He paused for a long time, and I was afraid he was going to stand up and head for the dorms. There was a low rumble of thunder in the sky. I kept waiting, and finally, he started talking again. "It was a long flight back to Phoenix. I wanted to cry the whole way."

But the best was when he talked about his playing time with other players, guys I'd heard of—Billy Bolter, Orlando Williams, Pedro Francisco. Even Jackson Alter! I told him Alter was my favorite, and he told me about the year they played together on the Phillies.

"Alter ate a cheesesteak after every single home game. Cheesesteaks with pepper and onions. That's something I hope never to smell again."

"What's he like?" He actually knew Jackson Alter!

"He's a rock-solid guy. I never heard him say a bad word about anyone. He works really hard. A good teammate. There's nothing not to respect about Jackson Alter."

I knew that. It was the kind of thing you just knew, watching Jackson Alter play ball, listening to him talk, seeing how he acted with his teammates.

"I miss it so much," J-Mac said, his eyes on the brightly lit field.

The sound of Ralphie-O's mower grew louder as it worked its way from the outfield toward the infield.

"So what happened?" I asked, remembering what I was really after. Not great stories. An explanation. A confession.

The happiness of those memories had been lighting up J-Mac's face, but it faded fast, a screen turned off. "I guess to you it looks like there was one minute when everything changed. But it didn't feel like that." He paused, kicking at the grass in front of the bench. "This might surprise you, Casey, but I didn't know too many guys who played naked."

I burst out laughing.

He shook his head. "Not that naked," he said. "No, I mean back then we'd all take some pills, you know, so we'd have the strength to get out there and play hard every day. It's not as easy as it looks."

As I wrote down every word he said, something was crackling beneath my skin, almost like a lie detector going off. *No! That's bull. That's just bull. No!* They didn't *all* take pills. That was a lie.

"Are you saying every player took steroids?"

He looked at me like I was some stupid little kid. "I didn't say anything about *steroids*. I'm talking about other stuff, like greenies, you know, stimulants."

"Legal pills?"

"Well, not exactly. But they weren't banned by Major League Baseball at that time, either."

I couldn't sit next to this guy anymore. I jumped up from the bench and stood in front of him. I wanted to get right in his face. "But that thing with Reggie Rhodes, where he said he got stuff from your locker, wasn't *that* steroids? And then why didn't you speak up? Why did you run away and hide?"

"Hold on, Casey. Slow down. It was complicated. Reggie Rhodes was a user. He used steroids for years. And he took greenies too, all that stuff. And, yeah, he probably got something from me. Not the steroids, though."

"So you're saying you never used steroids?"

"I'm not saying that. I'm saying he didn't get them from me."

I sat back down. "But I just don't understand. Why would you?"

He closed his eyes for a long time. The sky continued with its low rumbles, though I didn't see any lightning.

"It got to this point where if you weren't taking something—whatever kind of drug you want to call it—good luck keeping up with everyone else, because all your teammates were. And all your opponents were. Is it fair for a clean pitcher to have to face a juiced-up power hitter? It wasn't like you were trying to get some unfair advantage. You were trying to keep up with everyone else."

Every tendon and muscle and nerve in my body was tense and angry, because I knew what he was saying was wrong. It was completely wrong. You couldn't say, *I did it because everyone was doing it.* Rules govern the game of baseball—rules govern everything!—and you don't get to pick which rules you want to follow. There's integrity to the game. And the rules apply to everyone.

But.

I hated that there was a *but.* I wasn't even sure what that *but* was, but there was a part of what he was saying that I almost understood. I didn't like it. I didn't think he was right. But I wasn't sure he was completely not right.

And it definitely wasn't the story I had thought it was.

"So if Reggie Rhodes was lying," I said, "if he

didn't get steroids from your locker, why didn't you defend yourself?"

"I'm trusting you not to tell anyone this, not that anyone would necessarily believe you anyway. This is off the record."

Whoa. I put my pad down. When someone says something is off the record, there's no messing around. It's serious and important, like an oath: the person is talking freely, willing to say things he might not otherwise say. A reporter is never allowed to use anything said off the record.

"I wasn't exactly innocent. I'm not saying it was right, but I *had* taken steroids. I'd been off for a while by the time this happened. But like I told you, I was still taking other drugs, nothing big, just some little stuff, and so were a lot of players. The thing is: I knew who was taking. And if I came forward and ended up being questioned, I was going to bring down a lot of other people. Really good players. Good men. Good friends."

"If they were guilty, they should have paid the price." Pop would have been proud; there was strength and conviction in my voice. I sounded like the best kind of umpire, confident in his call.

J-Mac shook his head like I had no idea what I was talking about. "You sure about that?" he asked.

"No doubt," I said. "There's no place for drug-taking cheaters in baseball." I couldn't believe I'd said that to his face. I felt like a tiny mouse from a fable or something, taking on a giant elephant.

"So I should have brought them all down, Casey? Really? All the players I knew who had been taking drugs, I should have sold them out, named their names."

I nodded my head, hard.

"Do you feel any different knowing that Jackson Alter was one of the people I'd have had to name?"

It felt like he had reached down my throat and pulled my lungs right out of my body. I could not breathe in the same way I'd always been able to breathe before.

He shook his head, put up his hand, and said, "I'll deny ever having said that. I didn't say that, okay? Just — I didn't say that." Then he stood up and walked away.

Bottom Dropped Out

I JUST sat there, not sure I'd be able to get my legs to function how they were supposed to. I looked over my notes. I thought about what he'd said. And I didn't think I'd ever again summon the strength to move. But I did when the sky broke open and rain started pouring down. I protected my notebook under my shirt and ran to the gym. I stood there, staring at that sign: SURPRISE IS THE ENEMY OF THE UMPIRE.

And maybe it's the enemy of the reporter, too. Maybe surprise is the enemy of the baseball fan. Or the Jackson Alter fan.

Or maybe it's just the enemy. Always.

I paced back and forth, shuffling my feet to make that squeaky gym-floor noise, to try to drown out the grinding jumble of thoughts slogging around in my head. I had gotten the interview—I could write the article now. J-Mac had told me so much stuff. But when my brain even started to reveal the tiniest corner of what he said about Jackson Alter, I started pacing faster, scuffing more, making a roomful of sneaker noise.

How could I write that article? I knew I couldn't touch any of the off-the-record stuff, but still! He said so much before he went off the record! But how would it even be possible to be objective, to be fair, when I had such strong feelings about what he told me? It was all wrong, wrong, wrong. But still, somehow it felt like I was starting to understand what made him do it. While at the same time, I still thought it was wrong, wrong, wrong.

I finally sat down. Then I stood right back up and started squeak-pacing that floor, hoping some smart thought, some decision, some something would come to me.

But it didn't.

You Suck, Ump!

BASEBALL is always best on warm, sunny days. Even the kind of baseball that involves screaming wildly, loudly, and maybe inappropriately at umpire students. And that was the kind of day we woke up to on Saturday, You Suck, Ump! Day. A strong powder-blue sky, fluffy white clouds. Perfect.

I hadn't figured out what to do about my article, but I made a deal with myself to put that on hold until I got through this day. I could not mess up this day.

When Zeke arrived, I already had the big signs in place, and I was cleaning up the bleachers on the first-base side. "Did you do the third-base side yet?" Zeke asked. I shook my head, and, not missing a beat, he grabbed a trash bag and broom and got to work.

He was back in five minutes.

"Do you think your dad could spare a memory

whatchamacallit for the video camera? I have one here, but I always like to have a backup."

"You're definitely videotaping?"

He nodded, but he wasn't looking at me.

"My dad doesn't know?"

"He, uh, doesn't know that I'm not taping, if that's what you mean."

"I don't even understand that," I said, then realized I sounded like Sly. I picked up the rake to get started working the dirt on the infield. I had so many things to keep track of today that I didn't want to get too deep into Zeke's own particular freak show. Simple answers, Casey. "Dad keeps the extra memory cards behind the first-aid kit outside of cage three," I said. I'd bet he already knew that. He really just wanted me to say it was okay that he was taping. Which I didn't think I said.

I went into the men's and women's bathrooms, checking soap, toilet paper, paper towels. Emptied all the garbage cans so we wouldn't have overflow. And then I went to close the gate so no one could come in until we were ready for them.

✳✳✳

The line of spectators started early, and I could see students peeking their heads out of the classroom. Some of them must have heard about You Suck, Ump! Day from staff, but until you lived through it, it had to be hard to imagine.

I was nervous when I saw Sly approaching. What had I been thinking? Did I really need to think about entertaining this little kid on the busiest day of my life? But Mrs. G. had a lot to do on You Suck, Ump! Day too, so I knew I couldn't back out now. I heard Sly asking Ralphie-O, "Do you know the *Brady Bunch* episode where Bobby finds that weird little tiki thing in Hawaii and then they all have bad luck?"

Ralphie-O shrugged and walked past her toward the end of the entry line without saying a word.

I yelled, "You are not allowed to mention any *Brady Bunch* characters for the next two hours."

She put her hands on her hips and stuck out her tongue at me.

We were not off to the best start. Then I remembered what was in my pocket. "You know how you're in charge of making sure no one sneaks in any fruits or vegetables?" I asked. She nodded. "Well, I thought you should have this. But only use it if you need it." I handed her a silver whistle on a chain.

She nodded in a very serious way and slowly placed it around her own neck, as though it were as important as — more important than — an Olympic medal.

"All right, then," I said. "For now, stick with me."

I had to get the bleachers filled with people before students came out for their morning break. If I'd been a student and seen all those soon-to-be-screaming people waiting, I thought I might have pretended to be on the verge of vomiting and gone back to the dorm. But that was just me. This was the one day students always remembered about their time at Behind the Plate.

At a regular ball game, sometimes one or two fans would yell at an umpire, maybe a dozen. But how often do you gather hundreds of people together to watch a fake baseball game and get everyone to scream at the umpires? What could be more American than that?

I wished I knew how Steamboat had filled the stands, but just like with every You Suck, Ump! Day thing, I had to come up with my own idea. Zeke and I let in twenty-five people at a time so there wasn't some huge stampede, and that seemed to work. As people entered, Sly looked at them with this crazed inspector-in-charge glare in her eyes. If they had a bag of any kind — purse, backpack, cooler — she made them open it so she could inspect. One time she yelled, "Attention, Casey!" When I looked, she was holding up a banana the way a cop might show his boss a murder weapon. She pointed at the NO PRODUCE sign. The guy — I didn't know him — shrugged, peeled the banana, ate the whole thing, and tossed the peel into the trash can. You can quote me on this: When a banana is your biggest problem, you're having a pretty good day.

Once everyone was seated, we could see that we hadn't overfilled the stands — there was still extra room out in right field. That meant Zeke's bouncer duties weren't needed, so he was free to shoot video.

When students started trotting out to the field, some looked nervous. June Sponato was laughing; maybe she didn't know what was coming. Lincoln Cabrera and Jorge Washington were as goofy as ever, doing their crazy twenty-part high-five, which now seemed to involve bowing and twirling.

I stood near home plate as Dad walked out near the pitcher's mound. The crowd and students grew quiet. He talked into this weird old bullhorn. An overloud and unfamiliar voice said, "Thank you, Clay Coves residents, for joining us today."

A loud cheer went up in the stands.

"We hope you will be very loud and distracting as our students attempt to umpire a fake game."

Another roar.

"I will ask that when you see us speaking to a student between plays, you keep your roaring down, as the whole purpose of this day is to help our students. We know that for you, it's about screaming and yelling until your voices are gone. And that's great. It's why you're here. But we want a chance to educate the students, to point out what they've done wrong and congratulate them on all they're doing right."

At this point, all the instructors ran out to different positions on the field. Usually, drill practice involved a mix of students and staff—but today it was all staff. The infield instructors were throwing a ball around. Soupcan motioned to me from out in center field that he needed a ball. I grabbed one out of the equipment bag and was about to run it out, but saw . . . actually, it was more like I felt . . . Sly looking at me, waiting for something to do now that her inspecting-for-produce responsibilities were over. "Could you take this out to the guy with the big head in center field?"

She took the ball, then asked, "Which big-head guy?" I pointed and she ran off.

My dad was talking again. "We ask that you remember that there are some children in attendance. Oh, hello, Sylvia," he said, as she ran by.

"Sly!" I said under my breath.

Dad was still going. "Baseball language is not always clean, but do remember the little ones, and try to be creative as you scream at this year's students."

"Shut up, Sloppy Jerk Hat!" someone yelled.

"Like that, yes. Sloppy Jerk Hat is a perfect example. Thank you. We'll be beginning in a few minutes."

The crowd grew loud again.

Even in the past, before You Suck, Ump! Day was my responsibility, I never participated. I just liked watching. Well, listening. It was hilarious. What I remembered most, every year, was looking at a wordless, open-mouthed, howling-with-laughter Zeke. We must have been the two luckiest guys in the world, with full access to every part of the field and stands at BTP.

Before practice drills got started, I looked around. It really was amazing how many people were here. If you thought about it—how it wasn't a real game at all, just a bunch of umpire-school instructors acting out different baseball situations—basic and complicated drills, the kind of stuff they did at BTP all the time—it was just wild that hundreds of people showed up to watch. And scream.

When You Suck, Ump! Day got under way, I walked out to the bleachers past the first-base dugout. My friend Charley Haddon was off to a good start. "Hey, ump! I was confused the first time I saw a baseball game, too!"

Andrew deFausto added, "It's called a *ball* when they don't swing and it's outside the strike zone like that. Come on, blue!"

That was an old-time thing, calling umpires "blue." Where did Andrew pick that up?!

Leah and Marley, the girls I helped with their lockers on the first day of school, and this other girl, Jane, from my old elementary school, were sitting next to Andrew. We didn't usually get a lot of girls here, especially girls our age. They were mostly just yelling, "Come on, ump!" And "You suck, ump!" LOUDLY. They seemed really into it.

I stood there for a while, listening to them, and then to Dr. Farber, the eye doctor. He was screaming the same stuff as everyone else at first: "Wrong call, moron!" or "You call that a strike?" And then he started going off on his eye calls, something Zeke and I looked forward to every year.

"When's the last time you had your eyes checked?

"Do you even have eyes?"

"Hey, blue! Call my secretary and make an appointment — I'm concerned about your vision!" He sipped some water, then yelled, "Hey, ump! How many fingers am I holding up?" (It was just one. Guess which one!)

I kept walking around, listening and looking to make sure trouble wasn't popping up anywhere. A lot of people compared the umpires to famous blind people; those lines were older than Pop. I liked it better when they came up with new material.

There were a few big clouds in the sky, but the sun was shining bright and hot. I looked to see where Zeke was and spotted him crouching in front of the third-base dugout. Beyond him, I saw a man, a tall guy, with a clipboard on the other side of the fence. Reporters always checked with Dad or Pop before they showed up, so I knew it wasn't anything like that. And then I noticed the guy was wearing a Phillies shirt. And just like that, it was all so obvious: He was checking out BTP because Dad was going to use the Phillies' spring training fields in Florida this winter. Every time I had pushed the idea out of my head, there was new evidence, proof that Dad was really doing this.

I felt something big building inside of me, building fast, scary, strong. I walked out to where there weren't any people, by the right-field foul pole. There was an awful swirling, building, building. Raw—it was raw and building. When there was no room left inside, it pushed out. The strength of it, like the scariest howling storm wind, forced out this miserable, broken, horrible moan.

"Nooooooooooooooooooooooooooo."

I looked around, but no one had seen me. No one

had even heard me, because all the others were shouting their heads off at the umpires. And then it was like everything stirred itself together at once, all these bad thoughts a toxic swirl. My father leaving New Jersey — and me — behind. I couldn't stand straight. I bent over, clutching my stomach as the moan picked up words and carried them along. "I can't." Oh, my God, I was crying. "I just can't." Sound kept pouring out of me, me who was left behind because my mother had met some stupid loser baker and could no longer stand to live at Behind the Plate, because she hated the place I loved most on this earth.

How could my own mother hate the place I loved most on this earth?

I let out all the pain but it didn't lessen. I wasn't screaming at the umpires, but this low moan of misery kept pouring out, like it might never stop.

It changed form, but held a steady pitch of gloom. "Noooooooooooooooooo" and then the no had no *n* and was all *o* — ooooooooooo — and it wasn't just my father leaving and my mother leaving, but it was also the totally screwed-up fact that Jackson Alter was just another dishonest drug-taking fake.

There was nowhere for my brain to turn without bumping into another painful thought. This You Suck, Ump! Day, my first responsibility, would also be my last. It came in waves as it all became real—moving away from Zeke for over a month or more every year, thinking I was this stud writer and learning my article sucked.

I wanted to stop, but there seemed to be an endless supply of every sad fact I'd been holding inside, waiting to scream its way out.

I had no idea how long I was screaming. Me! Screaming, groaning, crying in the general direction of umpires, if not really quite at them. My throat was sore, so sore. And I was hot, hot, hot. My body felt drenched, my eyes were wet too. I wiped them fast and looked around.

That guy in the Phillies shirt was taking tons of notes, and I wanted to march over to him and tell him to get lost, to go back and tell them thank you but we were not interested. But that was when I heard a whistle blowing.

Late in the Game

EITHER it was the loudest whistle ever invented or Sly had whistle-blowing abilities that were way off the charts. She was standing in front of the bleachers on the third-base side, blowing her whistle and pointing. I jogged over.

I had really only given her that thing to make her feel important! She wasn't supposed to be using it!

Sly was still blowing it when I reached her — and saw Chris Sykes with a tomato in his hand.

Instead of letting up, even though I was right next to her now, Sly was still blowing and pointing. She had caused all other sound to stop. Even on the field, Dad and the instructors and students were all looking at us.

"No produce allowed, Chris," I said with the very tiny voice I had left.

I turned around and got Zeke's attention. His hands were out to the side, like, *What's going on?* I motioned for him to come over. He put up his index finger.

Sly wasn't waiting for anyone or anything. "How did you get that in here?" she demanded.

Chris showed us a big bottle filled with red sports drink. And lots of hard-to-see tomatoes.

What if he refused to stop? Would I need to throw him out? And then what? What would happen when I finished my new article? No way that was going in the paper, no matter what.

Before I could even start, Sly said, "I'll take that, thank you very much!"

Stunned, Chris Sykes handed the dripping tomato right over.

"AND?" she yelled.

Chris gave her the bottle. Then he and I looked at each other, like, *What just happened here?*

I shrugged and kept my mouth from turning up the way it was trying to, into a smile or smirk or some expression of pure relief that this was over and that Chris Sykes had just been schooled by eight-year-old Sly.

When it was all over, Zeke finally showed up. "What?" he asked. "What's up?"

All noise had stopped. This was not good. "Why's it so quiet?" I asked.

"Hey, you okay, Casey?" Zeke asked. "What was going on out there before? By the foul pole."

"I was screaming at the umps."

He looked at me like he doubted it. Zeke knew I'd never done that before. But what other explanation could there have been? He couldn't have known I was having a nervous breakdown out there, right?

Sly reached up her hand and put it on my shoulder. "You scream good," she said. There was something about the way she let her hand stay there, something almost comforting, that made me wonder if somehow she had really seen me crying. If I'd been more obvious than I realized.

But that didn't matter now. We still had a ton more students to go — like twenty-five pairs. The whole point of You Suck, Ump! Day was creating a lot of noise. A LOT OF NOISE. LOUD NOISE. And somehow, the year I was in charge, we seemed to have gotten ourselves an opera audience.

The students might not have noticed, but Dad kept looking around, like he was wondering what was going on. He and Pop and the instructors were standing just outside the foul lines. They were supposed to be evaluating how well students responded to the pressure of being screamed at. Only it was silent.

Dad caught my eye and shot me a panicked look, his arms out to the side asking what was going on.

"We need to get this going again," I yelled. "Hey, ump! You couldn't make a good call if someone handed you a phone!"

Lincoln Cabrera was behind the plate. He turned to see who was yelling junk at him after all that quiet. He had a pretty fierce look on his face. He tried to stare me down.

I smiled a guilty smile and shrugged, but somehow, the way he was glaring at me made the whole section sitting behind me a little angry.

"What are you looking at, blue?" a big guy growled.

"Eyes on the game, ump," the high school football coach yelled. "Not that it matters!"

"Turn around, loser! The game's in front of you, not behind you."

"Hey, ump! Wipe the plate! At least you'd be doing something more than just standing there!"

And it caught on—somehow a new surge of energy passed through the stands—people tried to outdo each other, to be louder than the guys next to them, more creative in their noncursing (and sometimes cursing) streams of nasty words.

"We're good?" Zeke asked, with an awkward pat on my back.

I nodded. My throat was still sore. I walked to the water fountain and drank, then splashed some water on my face. Okay. We had gotten through the hard part. The crowd was back to its roar, screaming at the umpires, telling them how much they sucked.

In fact, somehow, the crowd even got the wave going. A first at You Suck, Ump! Day.

All in all, you'd have to say the day was a great success. I had taken care of the whole thing, start to finish. Sure, I still had some stuff to sort out—okay, a lot of hard, feelings-y stuff to sort out—but this part, this You Suck, Ump! Day part, had been very good.

✻✻✻

Zeke stayed to help clean up the stands with me.

Sly came over while I was hauling a bag of trash out to the Dumpster. "Here's your whistle," she said.

"Keep it," I said. "You did a great job."

"See, Grandma? I told you I could keep it. Bye, Casey. And bye, you," she called over to Zeke.

He waved goodbye to both of us too, heading

home to edit the video he'd just shot. And I started walking back to my house.

✳ ✳ ✳

So imagine you were walking along, minutes after the end of an awesome You Suck, Ump! Day, whistling a happy song. Now, don't feel bad if you're not a whistler. I happen to be a great whistler, but I know there are plenty of good people—otherwise talented people—who couldn't whistle to save their lives. So maybe you were walking along humming. Anyway, you were kind of absently happy. It was a nice day, the sun was hotter than you'd think it would be in late September, and then out of nowhere, someone appeared in your path and kicked you in your most private area repeatedly.

While that isn't an actual description of what happened to me (I am a good whistler, though), it was what it felt like. I turned the corner to BTP, and when I looked up at the top of the stairs to our house, there was my mother.

I hadn't seen her in seven months. And that time was just because I was forced to attend my cousin's wedding, which I mostly blocked out of my brain because it led my memory to another wedding, one I never wanted to think about.

She was just sitting there, my mom. But really,

I didn't think of her as my mom. She was more the woman who used to live here back when she was my mom. She started to hate everything about Behind the Plate except for the baker who came each morning, and she became Mrs. Bob the Baker when she chose to leave. She chose that. And now I chose not to say hello.

I could hear the chatter of instructors calling out situations on the fields behind me: "Nobody on, nobody out," and then the crack of bat on ball. That was where I wanted to be. In fact, anyplace but right here, right now, was where I wanted to be.

"You're a hard guy to reach," she said with a friendly-seeming smile.

I shrugged. I didn't care.

"I just want to talk to you, to see how you are."

"I'm fine," I said.

I heard students yelling out their calls: "You're out! No run scores! No run scores!"

"When your dad and I got divorced, the plan was not that I would never see you again," she said. She was looking right at me, but I couldn't keep looking back. "The deal was that I had you every other weekend, and one or two weeknights when it wouldn't be too disruptive. We kept it loose and friendly."

She paused, the conversational hint that it was my turn to speak. But I had nothing to say to her.

"I never thought it was a good idea to force you to stay with me when you didn't want to. You were angry, and I understood that, and I thought I was doing the right thing. But it's gotten out of hand. The agreement is that I get you every other weekend."

"Even if I don't want to be gotten?"

"What's the alternative?" she asked.

I sat on the bottom step so I didn't have to look at her anymore. Not that I cared, but her eyes were wet. "This. I live here. With Dad and Pop. I don't live with you and Bob the Baker. I don't." That was a choice *she* had made.

"But you're my son, and I love you."

I stood up and walked into the house.

Slump

THE next morning started so quiet, maybe because Zeke wasn't around. He had to go to Brooklyn to visit his grandfather. Maybe we had all spent more energy on You Suck, Ump! Day than we realized. Dad and Pop said their heads were still throbbing when they woke up, echoes of all the crowd noise. And me, well, let's say seeing my mother took it out of me. I felt like someone had hollowed out my stomach with one of those sharp spoons Pop used to eat grapefruit.

But instead of being just a not-bad mellow quiet, the day kept getting worse. Despite my protests, I had to spend the day at the home of Mr. and Mrs. Bob the Baker. Dad was driving me there. I didn't want to be in this car, and I didn't want to spend time with either one of my parents, to be honest.

"You could be more of a sport about this, Casey," Dad said.

Not really. He could make my body go. He couldn't make me be happy about it.

"She's your mother."

"Is that supposed to be some magic kind of word? Because it doesn't have a lot of meaning to me. She gave birth to me, yeah. And then she left. She got to make that choice, and now I'm not given one at all. First she decides not to live in the same house as us, and then she randomly decides it's time to be some kind of parent to me, and I'm supposed to what? Be happy? I'm not happy."

"Okay," Dad said. "I get that. But you're making it sound like your mom didn't want to be with you. It was you who didn't want to be with her, right?"

"Once she left, yeah."

"And I think what happened there," Dad said, pulling up to the light at Clay Coves Community College and slowing to a stop, "is that your mother and I made a mistake."

I didn't hear that every day.

"Your mother never wanted to force you to visit with her. She thought she was doing a kind thing, giving you time, not making you do something you didn't want to do. But we both expected that you'd get over it, and miss her, and want to get back to some kind of relationship."

"Well, you expected wrong." I looked out the window at the 4-C soccer team practicing.

"But do you see what I'm saying, Casey? We made a mistake, and now we're fixing the mistake. It shouldn't have been your decision. You should be spending time with both parents."

It surprised me, the way this came flying out of my mouth: "Is this all so you have a place to dump me when you need to? Is that why you're suddenly so interested in my relationship with my mother, when you were happy enough to let me not have one for a long time? This is about you wanting to go to Florida for Academy, right? Stick me with Mom so you're free to do whatever you want to do." Maybe the valve that had always held in all my . . . feelings stuff had gotten broken when everything poured out at the right-field foul pole yesterday.

Dad looked into the rearview mirror and pulled into the faculty parking lot behind 4-C. "You've been holding a lot inside you, huh?" I could feel him waiting for me to look at him, but I couldn't. "And you've apparently been eavesdropping a lot too."

I wanted to open the door and start running away, around the parking lot, forcing my dad to run behind me and catch me if he wanted to have this conversation. But he would. He'd catch me. And make me have the conversation. So I slid down lower in the seat and tried to brace myself. But he waited me out. So I talked.

"I should want your school to be better, as good as it can be. But I like living here. And I like you being here. And I don't want to visit Mom because I don't even know her anymore, and I really don't like her, and I definitely don't want to stay with her so you and Pop can leave me here and go to Florida without me. And I'm mad."

All Dad said was, "Exactly."

"So I can go home?"

He made a face like, *AS IF!* "No. Today you start visiting your mother. We'll start out with once a week, but you can count on more in the future."

I tried to interrupt, but he kept going. "Look, the courts spelled out the custody, and she has a right to you half the time. This once-a-week thing is nothing. You can also try to open your brain to the possibility that once you get over the mad—and you will—you might even remember how much you like your mother. You might *want* to visit her."

And maybe Santa and the tooth fairy would come by with the Easter bunny and take me on a magical sleigh ride through a fuzzy cotton-candy fairyland, too.

Dad looked at me for a while, but I really had nothing left to say, nothing left inside.

"About Florida," he said, and then I could feel him looking really closely at me. I'm not sure what he saw, but whatever it was made him say, "We'll talk about that. We'll talk about that when you get home."

He started driving again.

I knew we were getting close when the air got that weird beach smell—stinkier than the beaches around Clay Coves. Mom and Bob the Baker lived south of us, three blocks off the beach, and all I really remembered about their place was the way that smell felt heavy in your nose. And also some really good muffins that she once had for me, covered with this cinnamon-buttery stuff. I wished I could walk in the house, nod at Mr. and Mrs. Bob the Baker, eat two muffins, and then get back in the car, but I was pretty sure that was not how this would play out.

"So she drives me straight to school tomorrow and then I can take the bus home and be at BTP all week?"

"Until next Sunday, yes," Dad said.

I hated the way I had no say in this. But for today

at least, it didn't seem like fighting was going to change anything.

I kept thinking about that sign: SURPRISE IS THE ENEMY OF THE UMPIRE. How could I have possibly prepared for a night at my mother's? What could prepare me for that?

Game-Time Decision

I HAD imagined that Dad would drop me off and I'd have to walk in and face them myself, but maybe he got how hard this was for me, because he grabbed my backpacks—the one for school and the one with my overnight stuff—and walked me to the door.

My mother opened it before we even rang the bell. It was obvious from her look that she wanted to hug me, and I hoped it was obvious from mine that she had better not. She didn't.

She let me in, and I remembered the place more than I'd thought I would. I felt something creepy slide up against my ankle and then I felt it on the other ankle, and I jumped about four feet off the floor.

"Oh, let me introduce you to Theodore," Mom said.

She picked up a handful of fur ball. Now, THIS was a kitten who deserved the name Tiny.

"He showed up on the back porch. We put milk out, and he kept coming, so, I guess we have a cat, though I'm surprised each time I see him."

I was waiting for Bob the Baker's big, stupid, booming baker voice to boom its big, stupid way into the room. But so far it was just the three of us, complete with very noticeable patches of quiet.

"So here's your stuff," Dad said, slinging backpacks off his shoulders at me. "I'll see you after school tomorrow."

"I'll be on the late bus," I reminded him. "Newspaper meeting."

He nodded and then, again, there was a look that indicated someone might be planning to hug me, but I managed to not-hug my way through the moment.

When he left, Mrs. Bob the Baker asked, "Do you want to hold him? He'll purr."

"Okay," I said, thinking it would give me something to do.

"I thought Sundays would be good because Bob visits his mother and then has poker night. It will give you and me some time to reconnect, talk about some things."

I nodded, but I was definitely not ready to jump into the reconnecting pool.

"Come on in here," she said, walking into the kitchen. The refrigerator was covered with papers. I took a closer look and saw a picture I drew of a rocket in the sky when I was in nursery school. And I had to look twice when I saw the one with my name written down the page vertically, like the one Sly did, the one I'd thought wasn't hanging anywhere.

"Would you like a muffin?" my mother asked. On the table there was a plate full of that kind I loved, and a big glass of milk.

Bring in the Closer

THE good thing I could say about Mrs. Bob the Baker was that she didn't push it. She gave me some space. She showed me the room I was going to sleep in, and let me spend some time in there by myself. I came out for dinner, and we talked about safe things. I did not like being with Mrs. Bob the Baker in her house. But after a while, holding on to the silence was harder than talking about stuff that didn't matter.

But then I somehow started talking about school, and that accidentally led to telling her that sixth-graders never wrote for the paper and how I'd tried but my article didn't go through. She gave my arm a quick squeeze, the kind of hug you might give someone you knew didn't want to be hugged, and asked, "And what are you going to do about that, Casey?" There was something in her voice or in how it never occurred to her that I'd let anything keep me from doing what I wanted to do—or maybe it was just that arm hug, or hearing my mother say my name while we sat at a kitchen table eating her delicious and impossibly sticky barbecued chicken—that was so familiar. And so good. And almost ... right. I didn't think she saw the tears that came to my eyes, and I knew she couldn't hear the thought in my brain, which was, *Oh, crap. Crap, crap, crap. I think I actually love her. I do. I still love her.*

Crap.

After dinner, I went right back to what she called my room. I didn't even help clean up the dishes.

That article revision was due tomorrow, and I felt a lot more comfortable focusing on that than on sorting through that crazy wave of tears and love that got all mixed up with my normal feelings for Mrs. Bob the Baker, which I guess were closer to ... well, nothing like love.

I had to get this article right. I had written seven different versions since I interviewed J-Mac, and I had thrown them all away. There were a lot of ways you could tell J-Mac's story and it was hard to figure out which one was right, or best, or most likely to get published. I'd always been determined to get that byline, *by Casey Snowden*. This was my only chance to get it right.

For some reason, this was what I kept thinking: If

someone told the story about the time Sly zoomed into the street on a skateboard and almost got flattened by a lawn-mower-towing truck, you might think, *What irresponsible jerks those guys are, getting a little girl into such a dangerous situation.* All you'd really know was that two older boys told a little girl and her cat to ride a skateboard down a sloping driveway toward a busy street so they could film it. I bet if Sly's mother wrote it, that's exactly what that article would say.

But it would depend on who was telling that story. And how they were telling it. The way *I* saw it, I was there, the first time, anyway, to keep Zeke out of worse trouble — by keeping him from breaking into J-Mac's dorm room. And I was there the second time because I felt bad for Sly when her mother forgot to pick her up after Brownies. If I were telling that story, maybe I'd have even mentioned how I made Sly the No-Produce Enforcer at You Suck, Ump! Day. And how she got a whistle.

It was all about getting a good angle, seeing the play, and making the right call.

But in umpiring, there was one right angle for viewing the play. With reporting, it seemed like there were so many different angles, and I had no idea which one was the best. Or which one was right. Or if best and right were even the same thing.

I pulled my notebook out of my backpack and I started to write.

***

I thought I'd have a whole awkward encounter with Bob the Baker the next morning, both of us heading to the shower or something, but I forgot the one awesome thing about Bob the Baker: He's a baker! And bakers start their day before dawn. I was asleep by the time he came home and still sleeping when he left Monday morning. Woo hoo for baker hours!

My mother drove me to school. We only talked a little, and it was a long, long way from comfortable. But when she said, "I'll see you next week," I tried to think about it the way she might, to see it from her angle, and it was hard to call her the bad guy for wanting to spend time with her kid.

Rally Caps

AT the newspaper meeting after school, Mr. Donovan asked, "Have you all turned in your article proposals, or your first drafts?" Mr. Donovan and Chris Sykes were both looking right at me.

"Oh, I have something," I said. Sykes rolled his eyes and started nodding in his sarcastic way.

I had pictured this moment, this wait-until-you-see-what-I've-got-here moment. All eyes on me. My hands tightly gripping the hard copy of a soon-to-be-award-winning article.

The reality, the now of it, though, wasn't that at all. "I forgot to hand these in," I said. "I sold two ads. One to Angelo's Pizza and one to Ralphie-O's Landscaping. They're both half-page."

"That's great, Casey," Mr. Donovan said. He

looked surprised, or maybe confused. Probably relieved. "Isn't that great, Tomas? Chris?"

Tomas said, "Good job, Snowden." I was surprised he knew my name.

When I walked out into the hall after the meeting, Chris was there. Waiting for me. "How come you didn't resubmit that article to Donovan?" I *knew* Donovan was going to tell him about that. "Don't tell me you decided to accept the rules all of a sudden." His words weren't that nice, but there didn't seem to be as much meanness in his voice this time.

"I have my reasons."

I didn't need to tell him that I'd written the story the best way I could. In my notebook. In fact, I'd written that story three different ways, and I still couldn't tell you which one was best. The truth was I still had a lot to learn. It was bitter and stinging, but it was the straight-up truth.

"But that doesn't change the fact that I think your rules suck," I said.

"You taking the late bus?" Chris asked.

I nodded.

"Me too," he said.

"So can I ask you something?" I said.

"I guess."

"What if we change that rule for sixth-graders, maybe for the kids who join the paper next year?"

He was quiet as we walked out the side door to the bus. "I'll have to think about that."

That kind of silenced me. I had expected some nasty response. I considered asking him why he'd always hated me, but it seemed both impossible and kind of pathetic. My dad had kept him from playing in a tournament, and he'd been mad at me. Anger isn't always logical.

Chris walked to the back of the late bus, where the eighth-graders sat, and I sat up front, wondering a little what it would be like when I sat back there.

✳ ✳ ✳

When I reached BTP's front gate, I had to look three times before I realized what I was seeing. There was a couple there, a guy and a woman — she had to be June Sponato — just standing there. But there was something really weird about it. The guy handed June something really fast, like he was scared of getting caught holding it. It was almost funny — they were acting like little kids. I walked a few steps closer and confirmed that it was June Sponato. Holding a cigarette. That Soupcan had handed her in a hurry when he saw me coming. It made me think of the reform-school boys who must have snuck smokes on these grounds, probably right here near the front gate.

June dropped the butt to the ground and stepped on it. Soupcan shook his head and walked away, like he was too embarrassed to even look at me. June headed back toward the fields.

"You can quit again tomorrow," I called after Soupcan, but he was still shaking his head. He didn't look back.

✳ ✳ ✳

As I headed toward the fields, Dad walked away from the students, mid-drill, to meet me, even though he was in the middle of student evaluations. That had never happened before, and I got a sick, panicky feeling as I looked around for Pop, but I spotted him right away out on field two, finishing up before break.

"How was your time at your mother's?" he asked.

I shrugged.

"I want to talk to you for a few minutes," he said. "Come on over here." We sat on the ledge outside the cages.

"I've been thinking since I dropped you off, and I decided there are a few things I need to tell you."

It sounded so serious, and I knew it was coming, how I was going to be sent to stay at my mother's. I looked around at this place that I loved, and I couldn't even breathe. Maybe when he'd asked how it went at her house I should have said it was awful, the worst night ever. Rewind! I needed to rewind!

"Overheard conversations are out of bounds," Dad said. "If you're listening to things you shouldn't be listening to, you're stuck with the consequences."

"Fair enough," I said.

"And now I'm going to ask you something, and I need you to give me an honest answer."

This did not sound promising.

"What did you know about Zeke's TV-show idea?"

How did he know about that? "Um, I did know he was thinking about it. And I knew that was why he was videotaping on You Suck, Ump! Day. It was his own idea, but, um, how do *you* know about it?"

"Did you see a guy in a Phillies shirt, a really tall guy?"

I nodded and I knew it was really coming now, the whole Phillies spring-training complex thing, moving to Florida for January, no more Academy for me.

"He was some kind of scout for some show about a new reality TV show, some contest Zeke entered. Your Show Here, maybe?"

"Are you serious? That's who he was? And he talked to you? Why didn't you tell me?"

"You had enough on your mind with visiting your mother. And running You Suck, Ump! Day. And I needed to think through some things myself."

Pop walked over and rubbed my head like I was a much-loved dog. "Everything okay here?" We nodded, and Pop headed toward the water cooler.

"They didn't pick Zeke's idea. Did they?"

"They're considering it. They were checking to make sure it was okay with me."

"Is it?"

"Now *I'm* considering it. I'm not sure, but who knows? Maybe a little TV exposure would get more people interested in our school."

I did not drop to the ground, but it took some effort.

"What about Florida?"

"I had already decided about Florida," Dad said.

"Oh," I said. I looked around at the fields and felt all the great memories — setting up roommate pairs with Zeke; watching students progress from spazzy to serious umpires; the big ceremony on the last night when they announced which students were going on to Cocoa.

"When I thought about giving up our New Jersey Academy, I realized that on a good day, it's more like a gift than a responsibility. Florida will still be there when you've grown up," Dad said. "And it's not like I'm suffering, being here. This is a good life."

My brain was revving like a lawn mower that wouldn't start up, ready for bad news, sputtering, ready to shout, "But, but, but, but, but . . . ," unable to adjust to the not-bad news he'd actually said. Suddenly, it felt like my blood was having an easier time flowing. Like there was less mess in the way of the oxygen getting where it needed to go.

"Last night, Pop and I were talking, and we agreed that this was one of the best You Suck, Ump! Days we could remember. You worked hard to make that happen, and you did it all. There are more than two generations of Snowdens, more than just me and Pop; you've got a stake in this place too."

Out past the fields, I saw Zeke on his skateboard, heading our way. I couldn't wait to tell him that Dad was actually thinking about his umpire-school reality show idea. I couldn't wait to tell him that I wasn't going anywhere, that maybe his real claim to fame was saving me.

"But here's what I want you to know, Casey: What I'm choosing is the whole thing. To continue Academy here. But beyond that, to be here as your dad. To be in your life until you grow up. That's not just a responsibility. It's the best thing I get to do."

There were no words big enough for all I wanted to say, so I just reached out and hugged him. Without a second of surprise or hesitation, he hugged me right back. I could feel some of the worry and suspicion that had been with me every minute the past couple of weeks start to fade. It really wasn't so bad that Dad had thought about going to Florida, so long as he'd decided to stay. And he had.

We were just patting each other's backs and separating when Zeke rode right by us, stretching out the word "S T A R V I N G" as he rolled past, heading toward the house for a snack. How did he know Dad had just been shopping for food?

His head was going to fall off when I told him everything.

"Catch you later, Casey," Dad said.

I was turning to follow Zeke before he had a chance to eat all our good stuff, and I nearly walked right into the massiveness that was J-Mac. "Hey," I said.

"Hello, Casey." There was something weird, almost like a question, in his voice.

"Thanks for talking with me the other day; I loved hearing your stories. I'm still thinking about some of the stuff you told me."

"If you're going to ask me to speak on the record about—"

"No," I said. "I wanted to tell you—I decided not to write that article."

It took him a while to answer. "I was starting to wonder if you were planning to bring me down or what," he said with a little laugh that almost sounded nervous. Or just uncomfortable.

"I really wanted to write that article," I said. I really did want to write that article. "You know, a lot of people would love to know what happened to you. But I was thinking that maybe *you* should write about what happened. If you decide to. Someday. What I finally realized is that it should really be your story to tell."

"But, Casey, were you—" A few seconds passed, though it sure felt longer than that, and he didn't say anything else. He just smiled and reached out his hand for a shake.

As we shook (let it be known: J-Mac had a VERY tight grip), he put his left hand on the top part of my right arm and gave me one of those gazing-right-at-you looks. It was a moment. J-Mac and I had ourselves a moment. There was more than thanks in it. It almost felt like respect.

He turned to walk away, and I took a minute to just look around. At this place, this third-best-in-the-country umpire school, with all its old reform-school buildings and fields full of people pretending to play baseball.

What a weird world my world was.

I looked out at field one. A runner was racing down the third-base line. I couldn't tell who the plate ump student was, but he was in perfect position. Beyond him stretched a beautiful field of green, still and glistening in the late-afternoon sun, and beyond that, I could see my house, my home. With his arms parallel to the ground, the student extended his hands slowly outward. His voice was crisp and loud and deep; it rang out with confidence:

"SAFE!"

Postgame (Author's Note)

This is a work of fiction. Clay Coves, New Jersey, is an imagined town, and Behind the Plate is a made-up umpire school.

There are, however, two umpire schools in Florida, and the method of umpire selection described in this book—with the ultimate evaluation and ranking being done at the Professional Baseball Umpire Corp. in Cocoa, Florida—is real.

Acknowledgments

So many smart, generous people helped me with this book in different ways at various stages. I wholeheartedly appreciate every one of them.

Olugbemisola Rhuday-Perkovich has always looked out for Casey and Zeke, maybe because she met them before she met me. This almost makes up for her insistence that Derek Jeter wears mom jeans. Kim Marcus somehow figured out that Jackson Alter was using before I did, and has held my hand through every draft of this book. Stacy DeKeyser gave me a wonderful weekend of writing and showed me where this story really began. Liz Scanlon and I wrote together daily, across 1,500 miles, and she's a kind of scary genius. I will always think of Casey and Liz's Ivy as literary cousins. Amy Hill Hearth cheered me on and met for Thai lunches whenever the need arose. Pamela Ross always wears her pride in her friends like a mama.

I worked on this book as a student in Patti Gauch's Heart of the Novel workshop, and she taught us all so much. I am grateful that she shares her wisdom so freely. My thanks, too, to all my Heart of the Novel mates for their feedback.

I want to thank everyone at JEAPU, especially Jim Evans and Dick Nelson, for patiently answering a rookie's questions and allowing me to watch an umpire school in session.

I am lucky to belong to two incredible groups of writers — the EMLA Gango and the Atomic Engineers. The support, camaraderie, and fun to be had within those circles is immeasurable and extraordinary.

My editor, Jennifer Greene, is all kinds of wonderful. Her always light touch invariably evokes deep and meaningful change. Any writer would be lucky to have Jennifer on her team. Everyone at Clarion Books has transformed my manuscripts into beautiful books, for which I will always be deeply appreciative and somewhat awestruck.

That Erin Murphy, who would not understand a Scott Boras reference here, loved the long-ago-cut parts of this manuscript that featured Casey and Zeke doing nothing but geeking out together should have been a pretty clear indicator that I'd found the right agent. This is the book that started it all, so I guess I am also grateful to Casey Snowden for introducing me to a great friend.

My family is large and loving and supportive beyond measure. They make almost every day feel like You Suck, Ump! Day in Oppositeland—constantly hurling praise from the stands. I cherish the love and enthusiasm of Jules and Barbara Glassman, Ellen Gidaro, Beth Arnold, all my aunts, uncles, nephews, nieces, cousins, and, really, all my friends and relatives and friends of my relatives and relatives of my friends. My people are such good people.

And though members of the home team claimed unearned victory in the searching-for-the-missing-umpire-school-notebook sweepstakes, they are the truest, best teammates a writer could ever hope for. My thanks and love to Michael, Jacob, and Anna.

About the Author

AUDREY VERNICK is the acclaimed author of several books, including the popular picture book *Brothers at Bat* and the highly praised middle-grade novel *Water Balloon*. She lives with her family in Ocean, New Jersey. Learn more about her at www.audreyvernick.com.